2—

BOOKshop
22B KING ST
GRAVESEND
KENT
01474 561101

New and Secondhand
Books Bought & Sold
Credit Given
All Your Book Needs

PRICE:- 2.00

The Landbreakers

One fateful day, the Birch family begin their 500-mile trek to northern Oregon, in search of a better and more settled life. But when they arrive, their struggle is just beginning: what hope can they have against the superior might of the advancing cattlemen? And, when Jubal Birch finally makes a stand, it is so vicious and brutal that the conflict tears the family apart.

Years later, when he takes a wagon train to the Powder River, Jubal finds he has been remorselessly tracked by Slur Tayter and Luther Hose – two of those enemies who had driven him away.

Now, at last, it is time for Jubal's fighting ways to return, and now, perhaps, he can find peace and redemption – if only he can live long enough!

By the same author

Ironhead

The Landbreakers

ABE DANCER

A Black Horse Western

ROBERT HALE · LONDON

© Abe Dancer 2001
First published in Great Britain 2001

ISBN 0 7090 6899 9

Robert Hale Limited
Clerkenwell House
Clerkenwell Green
London EC1R 0HT

The right of Abe Dancer
to be identified as author of this work has been
asserted by him in accordance with the Copyright,
Designs and Patents Act 1988.

Typeset by
Derek Doyle & Associates, Liverpool.
Printed and bound in Great Britain by
Antony Rowe Limited, Wiltshire.

1
Strawberry Creek

Somewhere between the Blue Mountains and Snake River, an axle of the battered scoop wagon creaked loudly. Then the body lurched, as one of its wheels dropped into a sandy rut. Jubal Birch called out reassuringly when one of the big claybank mules stumbled.

'Whoa there, take it easy.' His voice carried clearly in the silent heavy air.

The ploughshare and digging tools strained against their lashing and the tool-box rattled. Pots and pans which hung from the wagon swung and clattered against each other. The two longhorns hitched to the tail-gate bellowed and swung their heads low with fright.

Jubal pulled a big cloth from around his neck, rubbed it across the dust and sweat of his tormented face. He blinked, stared around at the vast plain through which they'd travelled. Ahead of him, as far as he could see, the land stretched ever onwards. There wasn't a single tree to break the severity of the parched surface. It was poor land for crops and cattle-grazing, poor land for anything to grow in.

Jubal bit his lip, swallowed hard. He retied his neck-cloth.

'C'mon gals,' he yelled.

He heard the faint voice calling from behind him.

'Jubal? You hear me, Jubal?'

He gripped the seat-iron and turned to drawn open the canvas flap.

'Can't be much longer, Margie,' he said. 'We'll find water soon,' he assured his wife. 'The cows seem to know somethin' . . . there's a bulge in their eyes,' he lied.

'It's Willum, he's so thirsty, Jubal,' Margie said simply, her voice quiet and laboured. Jubal could tell that despair was eating deep into her faith and stamina.

He glanced at the boy sitting quietly next to her, and his jaw twitched. 'Then give him some water . . . give him mine,' he snapped, irritably. He closed the flap and drew his whip, cracked it angrily out around the head of his team.

'Head for the water, damn you!' he yelled. The mules jolted immediately into a canter, and the wagon swayed unsteadily as it rolled faster across the hot barren soil.

Jubal thought of telling Margie he was sorry, but the team needed his control. He eyed the ground ahead of him for stone ridges and potholes. If he allowed a wheel to crack, it would mean a long delay before he could move on again.

He banged his heels against the footboard, jerked the reins impatiently. He stared uneasily over the sweating haunches of his team. There was water ahead somewhere. "Nothing", didn't go on for ever.

How big was Oregon? His mind wandered and he tried to recall something from his childhood Sunday prayer meetings. Was it pestilence and drought? How long had it lasted?

They'd been heading north for more than a week. Each morning the water supply was rationed as they watched the rising sun break infinity. But now they were almost dry. There wasn't anything for the animals, and the goat that was now lying in the back of the wagon only carried dried milk in its udders.

Jubal knew there was water, and he'd find it. He knew about hardship – how to fight it. Lesser men would have given in – made a go of it along the way. But Jubal was determined to tough it out. He was a big man – not tall, big. His neck was thick and his shoulders sloped like a bear's. His legs were great-thewed, his hands flat and broad. His curling black hair hung down almost to the shoulders of his buckskin jacket, and an unwavering hardness showed in his dark eyes.

It was his grit, his steadfastness that had won Margie for wife, and brought them all the way from Salt Lake City. Nearly 500 miles to seek and stake out new territory for himself and his family. Almost everything Jubal possessed – including a fine buckskin mare – had been sold to invest in the prairie schooner; fifty square feet that had been their home for nearly two years.

First it had been the trek north into Idaho, through rag-house towns of gambling and drunken gunfights. On the outskirts of Rexburg, and out of weariness, they'd mistakenly driven a stake. But it was buckshot land – poor and moistureless – unable to sustain more than a year's crop.

Margie was crestfallen. They didn't want any more than they were entitled to, just a quarter section that was fertile and productive. So Jubal hitched up again and the family set off west, following the Snake River.

They tried hard and in vain to make their settlement. In Twin Falls, renegade Chinook Indians had attacked the town in force and destroyed the crops. At Glenns Ferry, prospectors tracked south from the Sawtooth Range. For months, the hapless miners had besieged the town after rumours of wash gold had spread across the state. Then, at Payette on the Utah-Oregon border, they thought they'd found a home. But within weeks, a feud had sprung up between the cattlemen and the farmers. A veritable range war fought itself out across the land that the Birches were bent on farming.

That was when Jubal decided they'd be best off striking out; to withdraw from towns that were fighting to become civilized. He didn't want his family to be part of the resulting bloodshed. Margie agreed that, together, they'd seek out a more remote part of the territory where they could build their own life, far from the quarrels and hostility of other men.

Two weeks after they left Payette they forded the Silvies into the Beulah Basin. Now, seven days later, even weeds couldn't feed from the earth. The Birches couldn't find so much as brush or tumbleweed to start a camp-fire.

Jubal shouted, and the flagging mules sucked in great lungfuls of hot, dry air. Their hoofs kicked up a pall of colourless dust which powdered Jubal and shrouded the wagon. The longhorns heaved their ribbed shoulders, extended their necks as they kept pace across the water-scrape.

But Jubal drove on mercilessly. He was becoming worried for the lives of his family. There was no turning back, though. 'Go on, run, you jugheads,' he yelled hoarsely. 'There's nothin' more from me. If you want to live, run for it.'

Jubal slashed the whip ever closer to the team's straining flanks, but after a few minutes slackened the rollicking pace as he felt a hand on his sleeve.

'Jubal,' his wife was calling. 'Ease up, Jubal.'

He half turned, blinking the salted dust from his eyes. 'You've got to hold on, Margie. A few bruises won't kill us. Get down on the floor.'

From inside the wagon, Margie was staring up at Jubal, then beyond, towards the massive sky. 'Look,' she said, pointing. 'Look at the sky.'

Jubal had been so determined, so mesmerized by the flight of the wagon, he'd been oblivious to the land ahead. Now, he looked out across the heat haze, up at the sky. The reins slackened in his hands, the whip fell into the foot-well.

Far ahead grey clouds had formed. Beneath, the land was clearing as the heat haze shifted. Thunderheads were rolling south, straight towards them. The wagon slowed, and Jubal felt the first soft buffet of a preceding wind. A silver flash sizzled along the horizon and the sky boomed.

'They'll be the Blue Mountains,' he said. 'We're in for a real goose-drowner, Margie, an' it's comin' to meet us.' Jubal's voice held off from cracking, but Margie caught the relief.

'We'll get set for it,' she said, 'I'm coming out.'

'You stay there, wife. There's other things for you

to care for. I'm just about ready to handle this.'

Jubal loose-hitched the mules alongside the wheels of the wagon. He hammered two posts into the ground and stretched a tarpaulin from the tailgate. As he tied knots, the rain soaked him to the skin within seconds. The barren plain turned to muddied streams between the shallow gullies and stone ridges. He grinned, punched a fist upwards as the rain lashed his face.

'Now you get out here,' he bellowed. 'We'll get us all baptized.'

He cupped his hands, and as they filled, pushed them to his mouth. He pulled off his Stetson, ran his fingers across his face through his dry, matted hair.

He lowered one end of the tarpaulin, ran water into an empty cask. He filled tin cups, held them out for Margie and Willum. Then he watched them push shallow pannikins under the noses of the animals.

After a half-hour of the torrential downpour, every available utensil was filled with water; enough stored to last another week, Jubal figured.

The family travelled for another five days. The plain gradually lost its exhausted crust, with grassy shoots and small plants beginning to show their heads.

As they drew closer to the Blue Mountains, the ground lost its sandiness, the pasture becoming green and lush. Just before dusk on the fifth day, they came to a tributary of the North Fork. It was fast-running and broad, sparkling under the dipping sun.

Jubal turned the wagon downstream. He followed the winding course for another two miles before he found a place shallow enough to ford. He urged the team across, the body of the wagon almost floating as the boggle-eyed mules strained against the current.

When the mules felt the shift of stones beneath their feet they faltered momentarily and Jubal shouted: 'Pull, you dumb brutes, there's sweet clover waitin' on that bank ahead.'

With their coats gleaming, and in response to Jubal's urging, the team dragged the wagon up the shelving bank. Margie was sitting beside Jubal, her face shining with cheer and prospect.

They pulled up on the wide, gently-sloping bank and Jubal swung to the ground. He looked at the green spread, kneeled to uproot a tuft of yellow paintbrush. He scooped at the dark rich soil, squeezed a handful in his big fist.

He under-armed the pellet across the water. 'Margie,' he called out.

'Yes, Jubal, I know,' she answered quietly, looking down at him.

'That's it, wife,' he said slowly. 'Unless you've other plans, I think I'd like to spend some time right here.'

Willum was standing on the seat alongside his mother.

'Right here's fine, Jubal,' she shouted.

Jubal waved his arm, traced a line around a bend of Strawberry Creek. 'All this has suddenly become ours, Margie. I can build us somethin' here. There's wood for the cuttin' an' we can grow whatever we want. It's a well-protected spot . . . I like it. Just imagine. I'll make a truck patch . . . plant some beans an' taters.'

Margie climbed down from the wagon. She walked up to him and put her hand on his shoulder. She stood silent for a few moments, until Willum started clambering from the wagon.

'What's he up to?' Jubal asked, smiling.

'I'd guess he wants to explore some. Maybe he knows he doesn't have to eat in the wagon any more.'

Jubal got to his feet. 'Don't know what you've got in them boxes other than seed, Margie, but in the chest there's some tins an' a bottle a beer I've bin savin'.'

Margie nodded. 'Sounds like a feast,' she said.

2
Cowmen

The first year was long and arduous. There was so much to do, and only two pairs of hands to do it. With a little carrying help from Willum, Jubal and Margie between them built a log cabin. They made it from timber which Jubal felled from the surrounding pine. It wasn't a grand structure; one spacious room with a shuttered window on each side and cracks blocked with clay and straw. It was homey and snug through, and solid with a sod roof.

With a timber stake hardened in fire until it was like iron, Jubal fashioned a sturdy plough-staff. He cultivated and planted his crops according to the manual. He read about the work the soil had to do, planned the furrows to hold water during the dry seasons.

The pair of them toiled from morning to night, day after day, never resting. It was a struggle to survive, and the staple food-stuffs of flour, salt and molasses they'd packed into their wagon were rapidly dwindling. But slowly the small homestead took shape, the fertile soil eventually yielding barley and corn.

In the second year there was an abundant crop and their food stores were bulging. Jubal had taken a trip to Bakerville; a hundred-mile round journey to trade root vegetables for coffee, tobacco and lamp-oil. He collected a mail-order catalogue for Margie, bought a clasp-knife and candy for Willum. He brought back hens, and two roosters, who strutted their stuff. Now, nearly a hundred chickens scrabbled in their run. There was a dozen head of fat cattle, and in the paddock, the goat patiently cropped clover and sweet meadow-grasses.

There was even an excess of food – more than the three of them needed. But Jubal never let up on the land. His plans for swelling production became an unrelenting and single-minded obsession.

'One day, Margie, one day ... just you see,' he yelled. 'They'll get to hear in Nevada an' Arizona. They'll even be comin' from over The Rockies. There'll be so many of 'em ... swarmin' like flies on meat ... they'll build a town. It'll spread to the west an' east ... but we'll have the best land, Margie ... the most land. The childer'll get fat an' rich off it ... we all will.'

And Margie listened. She was worried, saw the craving in her husband's eyes. She was getting nervous, took to watching the developing character of Willum as he tottered about with a whittled pistol tucked into his huckabuck pants.

'It's fine territory,' Jubal continued, his fervour unabated. 'There'll be surveyors plottin' for a railroad. I can see it now, Margie. We'll be shippin' corn an' squash an' root food all the way to Chicago.

Trainloads of produce bearin' our mark. One day everyone'll know our name Margie, jus' think of it.'

Jubal had a goal, and all the time he worked, never stopped the dreaming and working.

In the spring of the third year, the Birches had visitors for the first time – a four-man party. The men were provided with simple, coldharbour shelter, but good food and fresh coffee. They took heed of the land, gave their thanks and departed as casually as they'd come. For the most part they'd kept their own counsel – no word of where they'd come from or where they were going. Jubal asked no questions, just accepted the company and set them on their way with apparent coolness.

But his mood changed as soon as the men were gone. 'Told you Margie,' he said, excitedly. 'It'll be jus' like I said. They sure didn't say much, but see how they took note of our land ... what we're growin'.'

Margie sat with a wooden tray on her lap, sorting maize seed. 'Yes, Jubal,' she answered patiently. 'But they didn't look like settlers to me.'

Jubal's eyes were restless. 'Maybe not ... but they'll tell about it, an' them that're told ... well, they'll tell others.'

Margie clasped the sides of the tray, looked into the distance beyond the creek. 'If you say so, Jubal,' she humoured.

'Yeah, Margie, you see ... they'll come all right. Good farmers lookin' for rich land. It's here ... you see....'

Jubal's words trailed off. His hopes were becoming an obsession. In less than three years the desire to create a simple homestead for his family had become a craving for land, property and wealth.

The people whom Jubal thought would come, did. But it wasn't as he imagined. They weren't the farmers he'd told Margie about. They were cattlemen. Mostly greasy-sack outfits of stubborn men, who'd driven longhorn steers across hundreds of miles of scrub desert. They sought grassland to swell their cattle into vast herds.

Like Jubal, they were dreamers, men who saw the chance of selling east for hitherto undreamed of wealth – fortunes that could be made in a few short years.

Jubal rode to meet the first of them, as a mile downstream they forded Strawberry Creek. His jaw clenched as he saw the longhorns surging across the swift-running water. He reined in his mule, watched as the cattle pushed and struggled up the bank.

There were three men, and they rode up to where Jubal was sitting silently on the home side of the creek.

A wiry, tight-looking man riding a dun cow pony, spoke up.

'Evenin',' he said.

Jubal looked at the man and nodded.

'I'm Dad Preeve,' the man offered. He waved at his associates as they rode up to join him. 'This here's Slur Tayter an' Bale Mullis.'

Jubal nodded again, very briefly.

'You'll be Birch – Jubal Birch?' Preeve wanted to know.

'Yeah,' Jubal said, after a short delay.

'We've heard about you. Seems like this is a good country hereabouts for cattle.'

Jubal eyed the men called Tayter and Mullis.

'It's good farmin' country, as far as I'm concerned,' he said.

Preeve looked at his men, then back at Jubal.

'Farmin',' he shook his head boorishly. 'Farmin's just scrabblin' in the dirt for gophers an' tiddy-cats. You don't see *them* with dollars in the bank.' Preeve glanced again at Tayter and Mullis – encouraged a laugh. 'Look at them steers,' he continued, as Jubal sat impassively. 'It's a mixed herd. Two or three years on, they'll be near to a thousand. In ten years, ten thousand. They'll be covered in lard as thick as the walls a your cabin.' Preeve kept his eyes on Jubal, waved his arm. 'All they have to worry about is gettin' fat. All I have to do is fill a pipe an' watch . . . gold on the hoof.'

Jubal's face darkened, his muscles twitched at the mention of his cabin. As Preeve spoke, he imagined the man's cattle wandering across his land – stamping down the soil – chewing up his crops.

He leaned forward in his saddle. 'Listen, Preeve, I ain't takin' to your manner. This is farmin' land . . . my farmin' land,' he said, his voice grave and cold. 'Now turn your herd back across the creek.'

The three men tensed and the thin smile disappeared from Preeve's face.

'That's mighty unneighbourly, Birch,' he grated.

Jubal moved the back of his hand across his mouth, looked upstream. He reckoned Margie was inside, getting supper into young Willum. He turned back to Preeve.

'That's the way I meant it,' he said menacingly.

Preeve shrugged, gave a wry smile. 'Well that's just fine by me. You'll just have to take your chances,

Birch. You see, these dumb creatures don't rightly know the difference between farmin' an' grazin' land. They have a way of wanderin' anywhere their bellies takes 'em.'

'You keep your cattle off my land, Preeve. I'm givin' you fair warnin',' Jubal said.

As Jubal spoke, the man called Tayter pulled out his revolver, rested it across the top of his forearm.

Jubal looked at him scornfully, thought of his old guns hanging on pegs inside the cabin. 'What you aim to do with that, mister . . . gettin' tired of hidin' behind your cattle?' Jubal challenged. 'Or you just noticed I'm unarmed?'

Tayter grunted, shrugged his shoulders. 'Naah. This is just for effect,' he said. 'Don't make much difference to me how I teach you to be more accommodatin' . . . more respectful to Mr Preeve.'

'Then put the gun away,' Preeve snarled at Tayter.

'Is it goin' to be all three, or just you?' Jubal looked easy, confidently across at Tayter.

'I don't need their help, or this, to take you apart, hayshaker,' Tayter said, ramming his gun back into its holster. 'I can break you with my bare hands.'

Jubal gave Tayter a hard penetrating look. Then he dismounted slowly, let the mule stand untethered. He turned around, looked up at Tayter.

'You comin' down,' he said quietly, 'or you waitin' for me to lift you from the saddle?'

Tayter cursed as he swung off his horse. He handed the reins to Bale Mullis, unfastened his gunbelt and hung it across the pommel of his saddle.

He faced Jubal, estimated him. Tayter was heavy set – as big as Jubal, but it was surplus saddle fat, not work muscle. He made the mistake of thinking that land work really was for gophers and ranch-house mousers.

Mullis edged his horse towards the two men, but Preeve held up his hand.

'Stay outa this, Bale, I wanna see how tough Slur really is.'

Tayter snorted with indignation and started in at Jubal. He made a low tucked-in charge, expecting to take Jubal hard in the belly.

Jubal swayed to one side, dug a heel firmly into the ground. He swung up a fist that cracked into the bone of Tayter's face.

Tayter spiralled down into the dust, rolled over and shook his head. There was blood oozing from his nose. Preeve grimaced and Mullis shouted for Tayter to get back on his feet.

The shame of being hit, falling, maddened Tayter. He snorted, squeezed his fleshy nostrils between his thumb and forefinger. He scrambled to his feet, made another run at Jubal. This time Jubal caught him with a swinging blow to the side of the head, and again he reeled from the solid punch. With balled fists, Tayter stood, panting, considering his next move. He spat, made a wary half-circle around Jubal. Then he lunged in again, the full weight of his body finding Jubal's ribs. He avoided another punch, got both hands around Jubal's neck. But with Jubal's build it was little advantage. Tayter took a succession of short, powerful jabs in his belly-flab and his fingers loosened.

A deeper frown appeared in Preeve's features. He smiled thinly at what he knew to be the inevitable outcome of the contest.

Despite his work-hardened muscles, Jubal felt the

pain in his ribs. He was breathing hard, but more from excitement than exertion. Warming to the task, he took up a knuckle-fighter's stance.

Mullis whistled through his teeth. 'You're right boss,' he muttered. 'This sure is fine entertainment.'

Jubal moved back as Tayter advanced. He threw two jabs out at the man's face. One caught him in the eye, the other in the mouth.

'You gonna stop this, Dad . . . before our man gets himself hurt real bad?' Mullis yelled.

'No,' Preeve retorted with a shake of his head. 'I'm curious as to how Slur's gonna break the churn-twister.'

Jubal couldn't hear the men speak. Blood was roaring in his ears and he had no intention of easing off.

Tayter spat from his split lip, cursed as he moved in stubbornly. Jubal was moving his feet, ranging with his fists, when he slipped. His boot-heel caught a large stone and he lost his balance. He staggered on the slope of the bank, then fell awkwardly into the margin of the creek. He spluttered, twisted violently as the cold shallow torrent rushed into his mouth, up his nose.

Tayter saw his advantage and threw himself on to Jubal. With his tough hands he forced Jubal's head back under the water. Jubal twisted, took in a great draught of water, then kicked out. Both feet caught Tayter in the shins and he crashed down on to Jubal's writhing body.

Jubal stretched out an arm. Using a thick overhanging branch of willow, he pulled himself up. He lashed out a boot at Tayter, wincing as his toe caught the man square under his broad jawbone.

Jubal couldn't hear the men speak. His blood was roaring in his ears and he had no intention of easing off.

He dragged at Tayter, pulled him half out of the creek as he found purchase against the willow. He yanked Tayter's head, slamming the front of the battered face into the lichened bark.

'That's enough now, farmer,' Preeve decided. 'Any more an' I'll see you hang from that tree.'

Jubal stood in the shallows, water dripping from his chin and fingertips. He smoothed his long hair back over his head.

'Any more . . . an' it'll be for you,' he rasped. He looked down at Tayter, saw the pink flash of water across the man's broken face, lost interest in the fight.

He put one foot up on the bank, looked Preeve straight in the eye as he spoke.

'My pa told me that threatened folk live long,' he said. 'Well, you know what, Preeve? I reckon he was wrong. While you're thinkin' on it, turn those beeves and get off my land.'

Preeve stroked his chin as Mullis went to have a look at Tayter.

'We could shoot you . . . forget the niceties,' he said.

Jubal walked over to his mule. He took the reins loosely in his hand, patted its withers. He looked towards his cabin, then back at Preeve.

'I don't think so,' he replied. 'You'd have done it already if you were goin' to do that.'

He turned the mule around in a right circle. 'Remember . . . keep off my land. Next time I won't use my fists.'

With a hand across his ribs, Jubal walked off and

didn't look back. He thought of Margie and Willum, wished they could have seen him fighting for their land.

3
The Warning

Dad Preeve and his men settled themselves five miles downstream. But, within weeks, more small herds were fording Strawberry Creek. In daunsy mood, Jubal Birch watched from a distant stand of trees. He heard the lowing of the cattle as they were driven to their new grazing land. He didn't make himself known; spent a lot of his time in between, brooding and splitting pine. He was constructing snake-fenced runs to protect his vegetable crops. But he'd created an extensive holding and it was a hopeless task he'd set himself. With posts and wire it would have been a workable job, but he couldn't afford the materials from Bakerville.

There was another farmer who came seeking fortune. From his covered brake-wagon he shook his head ruefully when Jubal told him of the cattlemen and the increasing herds.

'These longhorn cattle . . . they sure need space . . . trample the land too,' he said.

He was a gentle, good-natured Norwegian immigrant named Lars Hamerdal whom his wife good-naturedly referred to as Pilgrim. They had abounding hope, but in everything else were pathetically poor.

'It ain't much of a start, but you could work here ... for me,' Jubal suggested.

Lars shook his head solemnly. 'We thank you ... but no. I build us our own farm,' he said in his faltering English. 'Maybe we find something further along the water.'

Jubal recognized the determination, and after they'd shared a supper of squawfish and corn, he wished them well as the couple set off downstream.

The Hamerdals finally settled twenty miles away where the creek widened and forked. Nevertheless, it was some comfort for the Birches to know that there was another farmer in the territory, and Margie could look forward to a woman's company and confidence should she ever need it.

Shortly afterwards, Jubal took to riding his land for most of the daylight hours. He became overwhelmed by the amount of work there was still to be done – to keep his land tended. Then the dread of boundary jumpers became an added obsession.

It was just after first light when Jubal saw the first of the steers. It was chewing its way through a rich crop of his barley and carried a Pitchfork brand. The beast looked up vapidly as Jubal approached, attempted to move off as the lariat coiled around its heavy shoulders. Jubal made a hitch around his saddle horn and walked away, the roped steer following on a few paces behind.

Jubal rode easy, and as he crossed the open rangeland he found more loose cattle. Short and long yearlings formed small bunches, and all were close-cropping the grass, steadily working their way towards his own land. He rounded them up, drove them before him as he travelled.

The sun was dipping when he came within sight of the Pitchfork camp and he was pushing near forty head.

It was the first time Jubal had seen the camp. It was a makeshift affair; a short bull-train, with canvas stretched between the wagons. It looked like ten or twelve men who formed a rawhide outfit; ex-army, who'd invested their pensions in cattle.

As Jubal approached they all stopped what they were about, waited for him with open curiosity.

Jubal dropped the rope to the lead steer and rode up to the wagons. He dismounted slow and confident, stand-hitched the mule.

'I'll take some coffee for returnin' your beef,' he said calmly.

As the men stared at him, he added, 'Which of you fellas is the boss a this outfit?'

A short, black-bearded man pushed his thumbs into his belt. 'Who's askin'?' he wanted to know.

'I'm askin',' said Jubal. 'My name's Birch. Jubal Birch.'

The man grunted. 'Yeah, Birch,' he considered, 'we've heard o' you. The granger from upriver who don't take to cattle.'

The other men moved in closer, smiled grimly.

'That's right, an' these'll be your beef I'm bringin' home.' Jubal took a mug of coffee from one of the men, nodded his thanks. 'They were gettin' mighty close to my crops. One of 'em had already made a meal o' my barley, but that's 'cause you hadn't heard.'

'Hadn't heard what?' asked the dark-featured man.

Jubal spat the acrid, burned coffee into the ground ahead of him. 'I don't take kindly to anyone else's livestock makin' a mess of my property.'

'You sure got gravel in your gizzard, fella . . . ridin' in here unarmed an' with a mouth on you.'

'I've got a family to support,' Jubal said. 'My purpose is just as great as yours, an' I'll do all it takes to protect it.'

The man looked around him. 'What you tryin' to tell us?' he said. 'I'm obliged to you, but I don't take to bein' threatened.'

'This time I brought 'em back, but next time they won't be goin' anywhere,' Jubal warned.

'We'd take a dim view of any damage to our herd, Mr Birch, if that's what you're suggestin'. We can't stop 'em wanderin'. Some o' them cows are a mite breachy.'

'Fence 'em in. I ain't sufferin' on land that's mine 'cause of you an' your damn cattle,' Jubal retorted angrily.

'This herd'll grow to more'n a thousand head in a couple a years. You want I should fence 'em all in?' The man was curiously indifferent to Jubal's hostility.

'Then move 'em. Drive 'em somewhere else. There's plenty of room in this state,' Jubal continued.

The man stared at the ground, thought for a moment. Then he looked up as one of the other men stepped up beside him.

'It was Birch who saw off Dad Preeve,' the man said. 'He made a real mess o' Slur Tayter's face, I hear. This fella's no shave-tail, Rouse.'

Jubal glared at the man, who shifted his gaze, walked back to his mule.

Jubal turned back to the man called Rouse.

'I ain't gonna chew it any finer for you ... move on ... get away from my land,' were his final words.

The Pitchfork men watched uneasily as Jubal climbed into his saddle. They had time-earned money invested in their small herd, were suddenly worried about what Jubal meant by his threat.

'Mr Birch,' Rouse called out. 'You remember, we're cattle men ... not gunmen. Like you, we're attemptin' to make a go, an' we won't take kindly to losin' any of our beeves to a gun.'

Jubal heeled the mule and walked away. Behind him, Rouse Packman and his outfit were troubled, proddy at the confrontation.

For a while Jubal Birch's warning brought him an uneasy peace. Along the land that bordered Strawberry Creek, the cattle outfits took to driving strays away from Jubal's spread. But after dark, even the most vigilant night herder couldn't prevent the occasional steer breaking through. As soon as that happened, Jubal delivered similar warning to the other outfits. And so the seasons moved on, with only sporadic and sustainable damage to his crops.

Then the following year after the breeding, the cattle multiplied as Dad Preeve had said it would. The herds got unmanageable. Jubal ran across small bunches that bore the brands and earmarks of many different outfits.

It was after he'd suffered an intrusion into his precious grain feed that he carried out the threats he'd made.

He single-mindedly selected a heifer from each of the responsible herds and drove them to the boundary of his land. Coldly, he put a .44 bullet into the young animals and dragged them to lie side by side. He left them with the brands uppermost, and thrust a fence picket into the ground beside them. To the post, he nailed a board with a few crudely burned-in words.

THE PRICE OF TRESPASS. J.B.

Ten days later Jubal discovered that a large section of his holding had been run over, flattened and destroyed. From the extent of the damage, he knew it wasn't an isolated or chance incident, as before. It was obvious that a sizeable herd had been driven deliberately across two acres of tender food crops. It was the eye-for-an-eye retribution, from those whose cattle he'd put his gun to.

Jubal sat his mule for a long time considering the dilemma, his next course of action. It was the breeding cows he'd go for – they'd follow their straying calves. He'd up the stakes – shoot every animal that came on to his land.

4
Crop Burning

In the weeks that followed, Jubal shot more than a dozen steers. It was ruthless slaughter, but he only saw his livelihood dying if he turned away. He'd convinced himself that he killed in defence of his years of unyielding toil, for the continued sustenance of his family.

Then one night in late summer, abed and wakeful, he heard the restless lowing of his own small herd. He moved his head on the pillow, glanced towards the door of the cabin. Then he noticed the orange cast that was blooming, reflecting in the lowest part of the side window. He understood immediately and rolled quickly from the mattress. He was across the room in three quick silent strides, then he turned back to his wife.

'Margie ... Margie, get up,' he called urgently, while grabbing his boots. 'The crops are burnin'. We gotta go.'

Margie was full awake within seconds. She took a quick shocked look through the window, then called out for Willum. She pulled back the canvas screen and gently shook the boy awake, got him sitting on the edge of his bed.

She didn't want to frighten him but she didn't know what was going on.

'What's happenin', Jubal?' she cried. 'Why's the field afire?'

Jubal didn't answer, and Willum caught the measure of agitation in his mother's voice.

'Mam, can I come? I wanna see it,' he said excitedly.

Jubal turned from lighting a can-lamp and grabbed his son gently by the shoulders.

'If you put your boots on, you can run, boy. Stay between the low pasture an' the creek,' he told him.

Willum grabbed his small plug hat. He looked at his mother then back at Jubal.

'Yessir,' he replied simply.

Within two or three minutes Jubal had grabbed the mules. He threw Margie a coil of rope and they rode quickly. Willum was swishing a heavy stock as he raced along beside the creek. There was a night breeze that swept gently across the fields and Jubal and Margie stood the mules off a distance. Jubal yelled for Willum to catch up and hold the mules, then he ran towards the rolling carpet of flame. The smoke swept over him and he knew there was nothing he could do. As the corn heads shattered in the heat, he backed away, stamped his feet into the ground. Isolated beside the burning, he tried desperately to figure out a way of stopping the spread of fire.

The mules were crow-hopping with fear and Margie was afraid for Willum. She was shaking as the night filled with sparks and crackling embers.

Jubal ran from the blazing field. 'Over here, boy,' he yelled out to Willum. He turned to Margie who'd made a grab for the mules. 'Hold on to 'em, Margie.

We'll run 'em together . . . side by side. If we can just flatten what's left . . . make a path . . . a break between the fields. We've lost the corn but we can save somethin'.'

For the next two hours, the three of them pushed and pulled the mules; backwards and forwards to create a trampled channel between the crops. It was enough to stop the fire creeping into the main crop, although embers still spurted. They carried in the breeze, but Willum extinguished them easily by beating down with his stick and hat.

Before first light they sat near the creek. Margie was wearing a shawl over her nightgown, Jubal was in his long johns. All three of them were soot-grimed, smeared with blackened ash and ground dirt.

With watery red-rimmed eyes, Margie stared out across the fields. There were still traces of glowing embers close to the ground, but they were dying. She ran the tips of her fingers across Willum's forehead and looked at Jubal, smiled emotionally.

'That manual of yours, Jubal. Somewhere, it mentions burning the land . . . improving crop generation. It's not the end.' She sniffed. 'We can replant.'

Jubal was only half listening. His mind was elsewhere, and he knew that Margie would want to know more about the fire. He clenched his fists, closed his eyes for a moment. Fleeting images of retribution chilled him and he shook with anger.

He watched Willum climb up on to one of the mules. The boy was exhausted, but the night had provided some adventure to counter the tiredness.

In silence they walked back to the cabin. Jubal lit more lamps and Margie made coffee. Willum lay on his bed, but he wasn't moved to sleep and his eyes were sore. He propped himself on his elbows, watched Jubal and Margie as, worn out, they waited for dawn to break.

Jubal stared silently across the dimly-lit cabin. He was distracted, as the faces of Packman, Dad Preeve and Slur Tayter flicked through his mind.

Margie handed him a large mug of strong coffee.

'You've got to tell me, Jubal. who's done this?' she asked quietly. 'There's something you're not telling me.'

She held on to the mug as Jubal reached out. Jubal saw the set of her face, the determination to be answered.

'They want the right to let their cattle graze.' Jubal told the half-truth. His arms tensed, his knuckles paled as he gripped the mug of scalding coffee.

Margie let him take it. 'Who's "they" Jubal?' she asked. 'Some days you've been gone from dawn till dusk. Where do you go to?'

Jubal avoided the direct answer. 'It's the herds upriver. They're pushin' me too far. They want their cattle on our land . . . the best land, Margie. They're not goin' to contain their herds. Next spring it'll be worse. We won't be able to stop 'em then.'

Margie glanced at Willum, saw that he'd fallen asleep. She stared through an open window as the first streaks of dawn broke the darkness. She was dejected at the turn in her husband's once open, agreeable, disposition.

'We got here first. This is farmin' country an' we ain't gonna move over,' Jubal continued.

'Why do they want *our* land?' Margie didn't understand.

'Cause of the pasture. It's rich in feed growth . . . that's what they want.' Jubal angrily tossed his undrunk coffee across the floor, and Margie started.

'They call us hayshakers an' church-twisters . . . us and the Pilgrim,' he snapped. 'That's how they think of us, Margie. Remember what happened at Payette? It'll always be the same unless. . . .'

Margie stopped his outburst. She looked at him anxiously. 'You're not saying we . . . not after . . . we've worked for so long.'

'No, Margie. I don't mean we're gonna move on. We've done that. Hell no. It won't ever be *us* that moves on again. What happened here tonight takes care o' that. They razed my corn . . . burned up part of my life.'

If Margie had known of Jubal's cattle-killing, she would have understood his vehemence even less. She stood close, placed her hand over his.

'It's *our* life, Jubal. Think about Willum,' she asked of him. 'I don't want there should be a next time. We're better set up now to start over. We can even sell the crop.'

Jubal cursed. He leaped from the chair, walked across the cabin. He pulled open the door, looked at the water as it raced along the creek.

'We've come hundreds o' miles for this,' he rasped. 'It'll be a cold night in hell before anyone gets the better of me again. From now on. . . .' His voice trailed off in a cruel whisper; he was thinking silent, dark thoughts.

There was an awkward stand-off between Jubal and Margie Birch for many days after the fire. Jubal returned to the repair of fences and planting of the winter yield. There was no let-up in his labour. He left the cabin at first light, didn't return until sunset, day after long day. Margie didn't ask what he was preparing for, but she noticed that as well as the Colt that Jubal always carried, the old plains rifle was now missing from its pegs above the cabin door.

The next confrontation happened one day in the early Fall. Jubal had been tending the irrigation ditches that watered the rows of squashes and peas. He sat on the bank of the creek, making himself a smoke. He watched the afternoon shadows crawl from the clefts between the tangled roots of the bankside willows. The day was still warm, but far to the north cloud was massing. He got to his feet and stretched his aching muscles, saw bolts of lightning striking brilliantly across the Blue Mountains. It was well over a minute before he heard the low roll of distant thunder.

It was when he turned to look west that he saw the broken line of cattle approaching. They were head down, pushing their way forward through the middle of the vegetables.

It was what Jubal had been waiting for. He cursed loudly and snatched up his rifle in his left hand, eased the Colt from its holster with his right. He took a couple of steps forward on to higher ground, saw the Pitchfork riders above the waving horns of the steers.

One of Packman's men shouted out to him: 'You ain't gonna shoot *these* steers, Birch. An' don't expect me to get down an' match fists with you. I heard what you did to Slur Tayter.'

Jubal swung up his rifle, eased back the hammer. 'Then you'll get it in lead, friend . . . makes no difference to me,' he called.

The two riders exchanged a word, one of them made the mistake of pulling his rifle and firing through the cattle. It was meant as a warning, to move the herd around, frighten Jubal off.

As the cattle broke away from in front of the riders, Jubal fell to one knee and fired. The man caught the bullet in his body and it blasted him from the saddle. The second man was wheeling his horse away when Jubal's second bullet smashed through the back of his arm.

The cattle veered away from the crops, away from the gunfire and Jubal ran forward. He saw the man reeling, his arm hanging bloody and useless.

'Get your friend's body off my land!' he yelled. 'Drag him if you have to. Tell Mr Packman he can have dead cows or dead men. Tell him to make his choice.'

The pain suddenly flared in the side of Jubal's neck where the rifle bullet had nicked him. It looked bad and it hurt, but it was only a flesh wound and he moved his already sodden neckcloth up around his throat.

It was nearly dark when he arrived back at the cabin. Margie and Willum had been sitting on the step for hours watching geese fly south, waiting for the rain to follow.

Jubal's tiredness was worsened by the throbbing wound in his neck. He grabbed at the mane of his mule, swung himself wearily to the ground.

Margie saw the dark blood that had soaked into his chest and shoulders and ran towards him.

'What's happened Jubal?' she said, her voice shaking, body trembling.

There was a faraway, detached gleam in Jubal's eyes. His voice was devoid of feeling.

'They came at me with half a herd,' he growled. 'It was the Packman outfit . . . one of 'em took a shot at me.'

A wave of fear swept through Margie as she watched Jubal swipe a hand playfully at Willum, then stagger towards the cabin.

'Is he dead? Did you kill him?' she pleaded to know, following him inside.

'From sixty feet with the Hawken . . . you bet he's dead,' Jubal mumbled.

Margie gave Jubal coffee while she tended to his wound.

'Let's get out Jubal . . . before it gets any worse,' she said softly. 'We don't want no killing and the law's too far away.'

'No . . . an' we already got the killin',' Jubal said, his voice becoming constricted and gritty. 'I ain't runnin' scared from this.'

'It's not being scared, Jubal. There's Willum to think of,' Margie insisted.

'They ain't gonna touch the boy. You'll both be safe enough. It'll be me they want now.'

'Because you've now gone and killed one of theirs, Jubal Birch.' Margie slung the words at him. She didn't argue any more, knew it was useless to try and change him once he'd decided.

She took a few deep breaths, tried to fight down the fear and frustration that was biting inside her. The first big raindrops slanted across the cabin and she stepped outside. She stood for a long time, let the deluge hide her tears from Willum.

5
Earnotch

A week later, Bugle Hose reined in his horse and spat a mouthful of tobacco juice into the dust. He drawled at his brother: 'These slacks are headin' back to the home ground, Luther.'

Luther, a doughy, bloodless-looking man with short blond hair, followed the cattle with his pale eyes.

'Yeah. Maybe if we pushed 'em north . . . scare 'em up a bit, they'd soon find the Birch's property,' he said.

Bugle was carrying a rifle across the horn of his saddle. He licked his finger, ran it along the gun's foresight.

'Fancy a small wager, Luther?' he suggested. 'A dollar says I can shoot out Birch's legs with one shot.'

Luther grunted. 'You know I ain't got a dollar, Bugle. Anyways, the boss said to steer clear o' trouble.'

'Yeah, "steer clear o' trouble". . . I like that,' Bugle laughed. 'But that sodbuster shouldn't a killed Polk, and Rosey lost half an arm. We owe it to them.'

'There's a brand to be run on these scatterlins',' Luther said uncertainly. 'We oughta catch and mark some of 'em, at least.'

'And if Birch turns up?' Bugle asked.

'Mr Packman didn't say nothin' about not defendin' ourselves.'

Bugle nodded, grinned maliciously. He rammed the rifle into its scabbard, kicked his horse at the cattle.

The brothers rode around the loose herd. They bunched them up, and for a mile drove them north. As they approached the bend in Strawberry Creek, Luther cut out an unbranded calf. It skittered away and ploughed madly into the Birches' field of ripe wheat.

Bugle yelled as he rode. The yearling charged and swerved, making a huge patch of crushed wheat – trampled even more by the encircling Hose brothers.

Near the middle of the golden field, Luther built a loop and with a practised throw, brought down the little beef. He hogged down the animal and it bellowed, its eyes bulging with expectant fear.

Under Rouse Packman's orders, Bugle made an ear-crop. Luther unhitched the young cow and they stood back as it climbed, shocked and shaky, to its feet.

The men watched as the yearling ran back to the rest of the herd. Then Luther coiled his rope and walked to the creek.

He looked around him, then bent to grab some willow blowdown – catkins and dried leaves from the top of the bank. He placed some twigs over them, then went for a bundle or broken corn.

Bugle was curious. 'What you doin' Luther?' he asked.

The Landbreakers

'Gonna boil me up some coffee. But maybe . . . just maybe it'll smoke our farmer Birch outa hidin'.'

'Thinking, brother . . . that's why you get paid an' I don't,' Bugle said ruefully.

Luther was about to smile at his brother when a noise made him start. He got to his feet as a mounted figure came thrashing from the long grass that edged the creek.

Both men instinctively reached for their handguns. Luther's trigger finger was trembling before he realized the rider was a boy, his mount a claybank mule.

But they had more than a callow youngster to deal with. Willum Birch was his father's son – hardy, already resolute.

As the mule spraddled to a halt, Willum launched himself at Bugle – a fiery whirl of arms and legs. There was a quick flash of metal as Willum hit the surprised man. He landed with such ferocity that bugle lost his balance. As he pushed a hand out to the ground he gave a grunt of pain and looked down to see the handle of Willum's clasp-knife sticking from his belly.

'The weaner's stuck me, Luther . . . grab him,' he cried out.

As Willum jumped away, furious and puffing, Luther snatched up his rope. Quickly, he snapped out a loop that dropped around the boy's narrow shoulders. He yanked hard and Willum fell on his knees, his eyes blazing.

Luther looked at his brother. 'You all right Bugle?'

'Yeah, I'll live . . . long enough to stamp on this button, anyways.' Bugle winced, pulled at the small knife. 'Get 'im hog-tied.

Bugle was standing very still, his face drained. He looked at the knife in his hand, his fingers sticky with blood.

Willum struggled, kicked his boots into the ground as Luther pulled up on the rope.

The boy yelled, chokey and shrill: 'Get off this land . . . you dirty land jumpers.'

Bugle lurched towards Willum. His features were crooked with pain and sweat beaded his forehead. He ripped open his shirt, squinted at the small bloody slit below his ribs.

'We better get you back, Bugle,' Luther suggested. 'Think you're gonna make it?'

Bugle was breathing heavy. 'Yeah, I said I'll make it, after. . . .' The hint of a threat trailed off as he glared at the boy his brother was holding down. 'You'll be the Birches' boy,' he snarled.

'You get outa my pa's field,' Willum squealed, his tears smudging the mud on his ruddy cheeks.

'You're gonna have summat to remember me by,' said Bugle. 'Somethin' to take back an' show your pa.'

Bugle's face was drawn and ashen. With a low groan, he stooped and picked up Willum's clasp-knife that he'd dropped, wiped the blade across his pants.

'What you got in mind, Bugle?' Luther asked, unsurely.

'I'm gonna mark him . . . notch his ears.'

Luther loosened his grip slightly. 'For God's sake, Bugle . . . he ain't much more'n fryin' size.'

Bugle's mouth twisted cruelly. 'He's still sunk a blade in me gut . . . feels like it's pierced a vital. Drag up the rope, he'll be kickin' at this.'

Bugle avoided Willum's flailing feet, kneeled close to the squirming body. With his bloodied left hand he grabbed at the boy's hair, turned the knife blade.

There was a tormented pitiful sound from Willum's throat as the blade gouged out a morsel of flesh from his ear lobe. Then a smothered sob, as Bugle pushed his face into the ground.

'Now you can join your own herd, kid.' Bugle spat the words, and Luther backed away.

Then Jubal Birch was there, and the wound in Bugle Hose's belly burst open in a big crimson blur.

The noise from the Hawken shattered the air as Bugle's body lifted from the ground. He was dead long before he came to earth, a wrecked pile at the very edge of the corn.

Luther was still backtracking, his eyes and mouth wide at the sight of the tragedy. He held out his arms, stretched them imploringly towards Jubal. He stared at the farmer, who'd killed his brother. He saw the terrible uncontrolled anger that was inside the man – saw the certainty of his own death.

Jubal looked to his son.

'Get back to the cabin, Willum . . . stay there with your ma. Leave the mule. Go now, and don't stop runnin'.'

Jubal turned to Luther, who'd made an instinctive move for his holstered Colt. His mouth made the shape of a smile. 'Oh yeah, cowpuncher. That's the easy way out . . . but you ain't gonna get it.'

Jubal dropped the Hawken to the ground then swung down from his mule. He reached into the skirt of his saddle, drew a stock whip.

He stepped forward and with no mercy lashed out

at Luther's body, oblivious to where he sliced and cut.

Luther took the first stinging blows, then howled, crouching, pulling the brim of his slouch hat down across his face. But the whip caught his arms and upper body, drove him back, his legs slowly buckling. Jubal was relentless, striking out until blood appeared through Luther's buckram shirt. The man's body was becoming a mass of jarring nerves and pain.

Luther staggered, went down on his knees. He grabbed the lash as it coiled around his neck.

'You ain't whipping me no more,' he hissed. 'That's my brother you just blown apart. You'll have to kill me now.'

'I aim to, mister,' Jubal said, coldly.

Then Jubal heard Margie behind him.

'You'll not kill him!' she screamed, running at him with her arms spread. She made a grab at Jubal, her hand touching the whip, which was wet and slippery. As he pushed her away, she saw his bare arm; it was splattered with drops of bright blood.

Margie fell, and she clutched at Jubal's boots. But he stepped forward, continued to lash out at Luther Hose. Then he trod on Margie's outstretched hand, and when he saw her sprawled at his feet looking up at him he faltered, shook himself out of his frenzy.

He looked at Luther, the body of Bugle. 'They were cutting Willum ... like a cow ... they. ...' he stuttered, breathless.

Margie reached up and took the whip from his hand. She shivered as she felt the warm stickiness on her fingers.

Jubal stood his ground, panting, drawing in great

gulps of air. He clasped his head in his hands, felt the touch of wildness.

Margie got to her feet and gently pushed him towards the creek.

'Get in the water, Jubal . . . cool yourself . . . we're going home.'

Margie walked slowly towards Luther Hose. The clothing on the man's upper body was ripped to shreds from Jubal's whipping. The shock was crippling and he looked up with fearful eyes.

'I don't aim to touch you, mister . . . that's been done.' Margie shuddered. She felt it hard to look directly at the man, the skin of his face, neck and hands torn with rivers of crimson.

There was nothing she could do for him – her thoughts were for Willum and Jubal. She fetched the two horses, handed him the reins of one of the grey mares.

'He was cruel . . . a savage,' she said. 'He deserved to die and I don't know if I've done right in saving *your* life. Get yourself off our land and never return.'

Margie turned away from the man, as he rasped from stinging, cracked lips: 'Someone'll be back, lady. Mr Packman'll likely form a detail to collect my brother. You best get your shutters drawn.' He groaned. 'You tell him . . . you tell your husband . . . one day I'll make him pay.' Luther Hose squeezed his eyes shut against the pain as he pulled himself into his saddle.

Margie listened to his threat, curiously shocked at the mention of a brother. She looked back and watched him ride away, slumped in his saddle. Then she turned to Jubal.

'We've some talkin' to do Jubal. I'm sick of it all,

an' we've a son to worry about. He's not much of a child any more.'

Jubal was rubbing his eyes, coughing, shaking his head. He got up from his knees beside the creek, walked unsteadily away from the bank.

'That Pitchfork cowboy. . . ?' he started to say.

'You were out of your head, Jubal,' Margie cut in. 'That was his brother you killed. Now there's two of them dead. It's none of your fault, I know that . . . but over a field of corn?'

'It's more than a goddamn cornfield, Margie. I told 'em to make their choice . . . I told 'em.' Jubal's thoughts were still dark, menacing, as he started off along the creek to their cabin.

'I'm afraid, Jubal,' Margie called as she followed on. 'He said they'll come back with a detail. What does that mean?'

'It's army,' he replied. 'Means Packman's gonna clear up . . . probably turn a mite ungodly. I ain't havin' you afraid, Margie . . . in danger.' Jubal stopped, turned back to his wife. 'You an' Willum. You'll both have to move out.'

'Move out . . . where to? There isn't anywhere.'

Jubal was silent until they reached the cabin. 'You can take the mules an' ride west. They ain't got no quarrel with the Hamerdals. You'll be safe there.'

'We're not splitting up, Jubal. We're staying here with you . . . where we belong.'

Willum pulled open the door of the cabin and Jubal saw the dressing Margie had tied around the side of his face.

Margie knew then that her husband was right. She didn't fully understand the rights and wrongs of the conflict, but knew it was useless to argue with him.

She knew the stubbornness from Salt Lake City, when they'd first set out five years ago.

'How long will we be gone?' she asked forlornly, when she saw Willum grinning pluckily against the pain in his face.

'It won't be long. I'll come an' fetch you when it's over.'

It was dusk when Margie and Willum rode out in the small stock-wagon. Margie looked at the darkening sky, saw the geese still winging their way south.

She turned once to see Jubal. He was watching them, uncompromising and severe.

She made a good-bye wave, didn't look at him again. Willum turned away, uncertain of why they were leaving.

6
Men of Pitchfork

Through a loophole in a battened shutter Jubal Birch stood watching his land. The quartering moon would rise late, and he wanted to see its coming. He guessed that, as an ex-army man, Rouse Packman would want to get at him at first light.

He'd cleaned, loaded and checked his Colt and rifle, set out his ammunition. He hadn't stopped once to consider his chances of fighting off the Pitchfork men. He was defending his home and family, not contemplating the possibility of stepping aside or retreat. He was staking his life for the hard-won land and nobody was driving him off it.

Determinedly he'd prepared for their coming. He'd cut chinks in the window shutters through which he'd shove the muzzle of his Hawken. The door was even better – heavy enough to stop a minnie ball if not a buffalo slug. The cabin itself was about as secure as Jubal could make it. He'd opened up the chimney hole, knowing that powder smoke would soon fill the room if he had to fight for long. But Jubal reckoned that unless Packman brought along a piece of artillery, he could hold the place for ever.

There was a night chill, and Jubal lit a fire of pine cones and twigs. He sat silently waiting, checked his guns again, made himself cigarettes. Then he heard the cry of a whip-poor-will from near the willows and knew the men were coming. He moved to a side window and saw the movement against the low bank of the creek – a shadow that faded away even as he watched it. There was a dull click as he drew back the hammer of his old plains rifle.

He watched motionless as other shadows then moved through the darkness. He tried to make a count, but it was too dark; it was hard to get the number. But Jubal thought there could be a dozen of them – Packman's whole outfit from what he remembered. He grunted, wondered if there was more than the Pitchfork outfit.

As Jubal's eyes adjusted to the darkness, a lone figure appeared to gain ground on the cabin. It got closer, presenting a nearer target. Jubal exhaled, took aim and squeezed the trigger. Against the reverberating crash of the Hawken, Jubal heard an anguished cry, thought he saw the shadow fall to the long meadow-grasses.

Jubal's single shot had hardly died away before the attackers opened up. He winced and spun from the window, stood with his back to the wall as a scattering volley of bullets struck. For a full minute the logs splintered, the shutters breaking up at the side and front of the cabin. Then just as suddenly the shooting stopped. Through the hanging smoke, the cabin and the surrounding darkness turned deathly silent.

As calmly as he could, Jubal reloaded, flinching as

The Landbreakers

resin spat from the dying fire. He crossed to another window and looked along the sights of his rifle, which he'd fixed in a chink in the shutter. He waited for a flash from one of the assault carbines.

He fired off another round, but no one cried out. He didn't know whether he'd hit anyone, but there was no more gunfire from where he'd aimed.

From then on, during the long bleak hours of the night, there was no more firing. Whoever was out there, Jubal knew they were biding their time. They'd got him bottled up. It was deadlock, but Jubal had to be constantly on the alert in case they changed tactics and rushed the house.

When dawn eventually broke Jubal was weary and gritty-eyed as he peered through a crack in one of the shutters. He could see a wedge of land between his pole corral and the creek. But looming close to the willows, he also saw the outlines of a coaster. He recalled it from the Pitchfork camp, and knew for sure then: it was Rouse Packman and his men. They were moving in on him, taking shelter behind the small wagon. This was more than a skirmish or a frightener from Packman – more, even, than retaliation for the Hose brothers.

Cautiously, Jubal pushed at the shutter. The wood creaked and immediately he realized his mistake. Half a dozen carbines blasted their rounds into the cabin. Jubal cursed loudly as one bullet scorched the side of his face. He crouched down, looked up to see another round smash Margie's cheval-glass that stood in the far corner of the room.

After ten minutes, Jubal shook some sense back into his head. He rekindled the fire and pushed the coffee can into its embers. It looked as though it was going to be a long job, holding out against these men.

Throughout the remainder of the day there was speculative, pot-shot gunfire from Packman's men. Some were sheltered by the coaster wagon, others had taken vantage-points around the cabin. Occasionally, though, one of them would get careless. An unguarded movement, and Jubal would loose off a round from the Hawken.

Towards first dark, Jubal was caught again by a bullet. It ripped through one of the breached shutters, then high across his back. It was a painful wound, and it was difficult to staunch the flow of blood. Although Jubal bore with it, the shock and damage tired him, draining his ebbing strength.

Darkness fell on the second night and Jubal considered his predicament again and again. For the first time since he'd seen Margie and Willum off, he thought about what would happen to them if he got killed. His death was becoming a possibility – a reality if he took to the fight. He knew there was no longer any chance of overcoming Packman and his men – there never had been. His cabin was the hole and he had to stop digging.

Packman's strategy had given Jubal a distracted, sleepless night. Just before first light, his thoughts were becoming irrational. He was on the verge of drifting into exhausted sleep, when he heard a voice break the pre-dawn silence. He shivered, shook himself into alertness.

'Birch . . . can you hear me in there, Birch?' Rouse Packman called.

Jubal pushed himself up against the cabin wall. He winced as his back rubbed the timbers. He answered hoarsely:

'Yeah, I can hear you, Packman. I'm ready for one of your dog-robbin' pack to show himself.' He pushed himself to his feet. Through a side window, he strained to see through the grey light, but Packman was out of sight behind the wagon.

'The fight's over, Birch. We got you cornered, an' I don't aim for you to be killin' any more o' my men.'

Jubal muttered a threat, eased back the hammer of the Hawken.

'If I give my boys the word, Birch, they'll burn you outa there. I'm tellin' you to get out now.'

'Yeah, that's what you want, ain't it, Packman? It'll all be yours when I'm full o' bullets.'

'I'll give you a chance, Birch. That's more'n the law in Bakerville'll do. They'll hang you for what you did to Bugle Hose. You come out clean, an' you can ride away . . . take your chances with Bugle's brother.'

'I'm stayin', Packman,' Jubal yelled back. 'This is my land and my farm and here I stop.'

From behind the wagon, Packman peered at the cabin.

'You should a rode further west, Birch. You've spent too long with your mules. Now I *ain't* a stubborn man . . . an' right now I'm gettin' mighty impatient.'

'I told you, I'm stayin',' Jubal repeated.

There was silence for a while as though a hurried whispered conference was taking place.

'Birch. You've got until sundown . . . then we'll burn you out,' Packman shouted finally.

'I'll look forward to meetin' the man you send to do it.' Those were Jubal's final words.

After that, there were many hours of silence. Not even a bird fluttered along the creek. As the sun rose and declined throughout the day, Jubal's spirit withered. He stared morosely at each chattel they'd accumulated since arriving from Salt Lake City. He wondered about Margie and Willum, tried to imagine a future for them. Then the torment turned slowly to anger, as he thought of Packman burning down his home. He wouldn't quit, everyone knew that.

So he'd die on the front step – making a break for it – after he'd killed the man who lit the first match.

As the sun eventually fell below the distant horizon, heavy clouds were forming in the east. Darkness was arriving quickly when Jubal heard Packman's farewell.

'Goodnight, Birch.'

'Go to Hell,' Jubal muttered defiantly. He slammed a shutter aside and with his Colt emptied a cylinder at Packman's wagon.

As he reloaded, he heard a scuffle outside. He cursed, banged his head sharply against the wall of the cabin. He'd made the mistake they'd been waiting for. In his angry retaliation to Packman, they'd positioned him – sent a man to fire the cabin on his blind side.

Jubal sank to the floor again. He placed the Colt on the floor between his feet and clasped his head in his hands. He apologized to Margie, swore vile and vehement oaths.

Within ten minutes Jubal knew the flames were catching. He could hear them crackling, licking at the walls. He could see the glow from the chink in the side window.

When the heat increased, he took off his neckcloth and dipped it in a water jug. He wiped his face and retied it around his forehead, accepted that

Packman was going to win. There was no escape. The flames were now curling along the edges of the sod roof. He wondered if that too, would burn.

As Jubal resigned himself to defeat, he fleetingly considered Packman's offer. But it was only fleetingly. Jubal Birch's life had never been one of compromise.

He calmly checked the actions of his guns. He still had a choice, and being burned alive wasn't one of them – he wouldn't die without a fight. More than one cowman would pay the ultimate price for being on his land.

He looked up at the roof, saw flames encircling the chimney hole. The smoke reached down, curled thick on the inside of the cabin. His eyes were prickly with sweat and heat and he coughed.

He unlatched the door and stood there, holding the Hawken, in his left hand. He gripped the Colt and thought for a second, let the Hawken drop. He wondered how many he'd take with him, how far he'd get.

The cattlemen were waiting. They knew it wouldn't be long before Jubal Birch broke through the door of his cabin. Flames from the roof and walls of the timbered dwelling were surging into the night sky.

From behind the wagon, Rouse Packman was steadfast and watchful. 'Won't be long,' he said. 'Must be an inferno in there.'

As well as most of the Pitchfork hands, Dad Preeve and Bale Mullis were gathered on Jubal Birch's land. But they'd accepted Packman as their leader. As an ex-army captain, it was he who'd finally decided to bring the offensive.

Packman's men had been hardened by army life, but in the main it had been lawful, honourable work. Slur Tayter, Rosey Mangle and Luther Hose had personal grievances to settle, but most of the others would, in their own way, have upheld Jubal Birch's right to defend his home and family.

'If he comes out slingin' lead, cut him down. But if he's unarmed, let him be,' Packman instructed his men.

The men trained their guns on the cabin and for a short while pondered on the engagement. There was a crude, imbalanced justice about Packman's decision. They were all angered by the demented beatings Jubal Birch had meted out. But, after what Luther Hose had told them, they weren't too bothered about the death of his brother, Bugle. They didn't hold with the wanton mutilation of a child.

However, they were now facing up to the problem of Jubal Birch. The cattlemen knew that Strawberry Creek didn't have the reach for beef *and* crops. If one of them had to go, then it would be the weakest – the one with the least resources. Jubal Birch had his temper, his fists and his guns. But he lacked the poke and manpower that money buys. They'd heard Packman offer him a way out, but if the man wanted to join his crops, he could.

The men were so rapt, watching the blaze, waiting for Jubal Birch to appear before them, that they didn't notice Lars Hamerdal's mare and its rider. From beneath the flames, the searing heat was splitting the logs of the cabin – the noise engulfing all other sound.

Dad Preeve turned. Keeping low, he ran to grab the reins as the horse galloped up to the coaster wagon. He pushed his Colt back into his holster, used both hands to control the mare, pulling its head down.

Rouse Packman was torn between watching the cabin and Preeve's encounter. But in the glimmer from the flames he could see who it was. 'Ssssweet . . . Jesus,' he stammered, recognizing Birch's wife, Margie.

Preeve reached out an arm, but she flung herself from the horse. She gripped the tail-gate of the wagon, staring at the blazing inferno of the cabin.

'Where is he? Where's Jubal?' she rasped breathlessly.

'We're . . . he's . . . he won't. . . .' Packman was tongue-tied, unable to react.

Margie grabbed his coat and started shaking him. 'He's in there?' she cried. She punched him hard in the chest. 'What are you doing here? Where's Jubal? What have you done?' She started to sob uncontrollably.

Preeve choked. 'He's in there, ma'am . . . still in the cabin.'

Margie made a long piercing scream and ran for the front of the cabin.

'Jubal, it's me . . . come out . . . I've come back . . . Jubal . . . Jubal,' she yelled, the words rattling from her throat.

One of the men made a move to go after her, but Packman held him back.

'Leave her,' he said. 'He'll come out now . . . if he's still alive.'

The men watched Margie as she ran desperately towards the cabin. They gasped, gripped their guns, as with a great explosion of sparks and flying embers, the door crashed open.

Margie was outlined by the billowing flame, faltering from the heat, when Jubal Birch stumbled on to the step. His eyes were blinded by smoke and fumes, and he fired in vain, blindly into the night

'Don't shoot,' yelled Packman over the gunfire. But he was too late.

His men sent a single, tight volley before Jubal touched ground outside the cabin. They saw the farm man throw up his arms as he saw his wife; they saw her, too, stretching out to her husband. They cursed in unison when their bullets struck.

Margie staggered, and Jubal threw his Colt to the ground as he rushed to meet her. Before Preeve and Packman got half-way to them, Jubal was cradling her in his arms.

The men stopped running and stared at each other, shaking their heads. With a ragged choke in her voice, they heard Margie say:

'I came back, Jubal. Me an' Willum, we. . . .'

As she closed her eyes her last words drifted off, and a strange, wild look cloaked Jubal's face.

More men had come forward. But they stood off, uneasy, as Jubal held her, as he carried her away from the inferno that had been their home. He made it to the creek, kneeled in the bankside grasses.

The Pitchfork hands looked to their leaders as he approached the couple.

Packman waited a moment before speaking.

'We never wanted this, Birch,' he said. 'It was you we came for. My men aren't to blame.'

Jubal looked out across the silvery, fast-running water.

'I know it,' he murmured oddly. 'You alone carry that responsibility, Packman.'

Jubal didn't say any more. He remained very still, staring into the darkness, watching the reflections of the flames dance across the creek.

One of the men picked up Jubal's Colt. Feeling the cramp of guilt, he glanced blankly at the cabin, then at Packman. His look betrayed the guilt of complicity, though he knew he hadn't been one of those who'd fired when Jubal came through the door.

Packman looked uncomfortably at Jubal.

'Whatever you're thinkin', Birch, it's over now,' he said. 'We're gonna pull back a bit. If you need any help with. . . .'

Dad Preeve touched him on the arm, suggesting he'd said enough.

But Jubal hadn't heard Packman speak. He was staring hard into Margie's face. It was as though he was looking for a sign, an expression of forgiveness. But nothing happened, and it created a change within him. Deep inside, something was breaking up.

Rouse Packman knew then that he'd fired off something formidable, that Jubal Birch had become a looming shadow of trouble. He turned thoughtfully to Dad Preeve.

'We'll leave him be,' he said. 'Tell the boys to bunch up Birch's livestock, then they can ride out. You an' me . . . we'll stick around till mornin'.'

7
Up in Smoke

Throughout the long night the log cabin that had been a home for Jubal and Margie Birch had burned to the ground. As darkness lifted, Packman and Preeve watched clouds of soft ash drift across Strawberry Creek. For many hours they'd sat with their backs against a wagon-wheel. They talked quietly, smoked and drank whiskey. Occasionally they looked to Jubal, who'd kept a silent and eerie vigil beside his dead wife.

Shortly after first light Jubal started to dig a grave alongside the creek bank. Once, he looked at the two cattlemen and Packman felt little relief in knowing the man was unarmed. Jubal took two hours in his heart-rending task, before finally laying down flat stones from the creek bed. He walked slowly to the smoking ruins of the cabin and for a while poked around in the embers. Then he returned to the grave with a tiny shoe-buckle. He placed it on top of the stones and nodded with numb, severed emotion.

Packman could see the grief, feel the hostility. There was something that was not quite human now about Jubal Birch.

Standing beside Preeve, he watched as Jubal walked to the small stock-wagon that Margie had driven back. Jubal climbed on to the seat and sat there staring ahead of him. He seemed to be totally unaware of the presence of Packman and Preeve.

Packman said something to Preeve and walked slowly forward.

Jubal turned, and Packman found himself gazing into cruel, purblind eyes.

'I'd tear your heart out from where you stood, if it'd bring Margie back,' Jubal said.

Packman shivered. Sweat prickled, ran icily between his shoulder-blades.

Jubal stared down at him. 'Give me my gun. It's all I'll be takin' from here.'

Packman recognized the undeniable request. He felt no real danger. Except for the words, Jubal Birch suddenly looked like a dead man. He glanced at Preeve, nodded for him to retrieve Jubal's Colt from the back of their coaster.

'You got a kid somewhere. Where you headed?' he asked.

'What's it matter to you?'

'There's a few o' my boys won't sleep too easy wondering if you're out there. You ain't likely to forget this night.'

Jubal didn't answer right away, just watched Preeve as he approached with the Colt. Preeve handed the gun to Packman who saw that it still held two full chambers.

Packman handed up the big, old .44 and Jubal eased back the hammer, turned the cylinder. He glanced at Packman and Preeve and smiled without feeling, let the hammer down slowly.

'Fear's a mighty strange thing, Packman,' he said eventually. 'I'm the reason for it, an' I *will* be out there . . . somewhere.'

Packman took a deep breath. 'You still got a boy to look out for,' he continued.

Jubal's eyes were bloodshot, and his face was raw, blackened with smoke. His clothes were worn ragged and bloodstained, but Packman sensed a hard-line soul within the beaten farmer.

'You got my land, my animals an' my crops, Packman. They must be worth somethin'. Take 'em. Give their worth to Lar Hamerdal. It'll pay for the boy's keep until he's old enough to fill his own belly. Won't be more'n two or three years.'

'You're leavin' the boy . . . your own kin?' Packman was puzzled.

'Yeah. My prospects don't offer much. The Hamerdals are good folk. They'll bring him up better'n. . . .' Jubal faltered for a second, 'he'll have a chance with them. Maybe one day he'll make somethin' of hisself.'

Jubal reached for the reins, held them loosely in his big, dirty hands. 'You owe me mister,' he said firmly. Then, with more feeling, 'Tell him his ma . . . tell him somethin'.'

'I'll tell him, Birch. I can see you ain't got it in you.'

'The boy's been hurt too much already. An' if there was anythin' left in me, Packman, I'd blow a hole in you an' Preeve right now.'

'Your boy deserves. . . .'

Packman didn't say any more because without further words Jubal flicked the reins and turned the wagon. He forded the creek, then headed towards distant Utah and the Buelah Basin.

The two cattlemen stood and watched as Jubal Birch took the trail he'd come in on five years before.

Preeve raised a hand to shield himself against the rising sun. He watched as Jubal galloped steadily east. He gave a loud sigh and spat at his feet.

'I reckon there's none of us need worry about him again, Rouse.'

'Maybe, Dad ... maybe. But you saw his face. There's folk somewhere who's gonna need to.'

8
Cobre Wells

The forage-hound had spent all of the morning failing to take a rat or gopher-snake. Panting, and with its tongue lolling it sat outside the hardware store. Anxiously, it waited for a handful of fatty morsels or biscuit that the owner sometimes tossed it at midday. But that was still an hour off. At this hour, most folk kept off the heat of the street.

Suddenly the dog seemed to forget its hunger and turned away from the store. Its ears flicked forward, and it trembled as it looked nervously along the main street. Nothing moved in the brilliant light but the dog wasn't comforted. It slunk under the boardwalk that fronted the store. It stayed concealed, deep in the shadows. then it raised its head and gave a yelp and a long, low growl.

Within two minutes, three old gold-miners stepped from a clapboarded building. Outside hung a painted sign which read: MOOSE DOOGLE'S ROOMS. $1 NIGHTLY.

The men bunched in the doorway, their old bones

aching and stiff. They shuffled, blinking against the high sun. One of them waved his hand at the pungent smoke of his corncob pipe.

'Somethin's up with that pesky hound,' he said. 'It knows better'n to yap at this time o' the day.'

Then, almost at the same moment, something else caught his attention. He stomped further on to the boardwalk, peered up the street.

Turning back to his colleagues, he shook his head.

'Freighters,' he said. 'Two fellas ... don't know 'em.'

'Cobre Wells,' the driver coughed and yelled above the racket of the freight-wagon. 'Ugliest goddam hole on the face o' the earth. But after a bottle o' Moose's bug juice, who gives a damn.'

Jubal Birch rolled on the sprung seat, easing the hard jolting of the rutted road. He sensed the driver looking at him and turned his head.

'Talkative son of a bitch, ain't you, mister?' the man growled.

'When there's somethin' needs sayin' I'll say it,' Jubal pitched back.

The driver grunted, spat a gob of juice over the far side of the wagon.

'No mind,' he cackled. 'Rode with a skinner once, never said a word for three days. Found out later he'd had his tongue bitten off by an Injun woman.'

Jubal turned back to the town. All of it was built of sod-walled or green lumber-framed structures. The windows of those buildings that had them were layered with yellow dust blown straight off the Silvies.

The dog gave a low growl, slung its tail between its legs. It slunk further back under the boardwalk as the

The Landbreakers

freighter pulled up outside the Moose Saloon.

The old miner eyed Jubal Birch. But he didn't favour what he saw and dropped his eyes, looked elsewhere.

Jubal slung his blanket-roll and slicker over one shoulder before swinging to the ground. The driver spat again and shrugged. He swung his whip and the team lurched forward.

Jubal hoisted the bundle higher on his shoulder and moved to the boardwalk. For a moment he watched the freighter as it moved off along the street. He was wearing rough canvas trousers, a rancher's blue shirt and a frayed buckskin jacket. His battered hat was coated with dust, his face was weather-creased, dirty and unshaven.

Deep in his pocket he fingered a silver dollar, then he quietly pushed open the doors of the saloon. Immediately, the warm moist air of the place closed around him. It was sweltering inside and smelled of sour beer, but after the glare of the sun the shade was welcome.

Aside from four men sitting at a green-topped poker table, the room was almost empty. Behind the long bar that ran the length of the room, a single bartender was drying glasses, setting them up on the back bar. Damp towels covered the lunch fixings; keeping off flies in anticipation of the trade: cowboys, miners and freighters who'd pass through within the next few hours.

The man grinned and nodded. 'Drink? Beer an' whiskey,' he suggested.

Jubal shook his head deliberately as another man caught his eye. Against the far wall a one-armed gambler was sitting on a high stool behind a blackjack table. He was idly flipping a pack of cards.

Jubal watched the careless movements of the gambler's fingers for a moment, rubbing at the scar on the side of his neck. He hesitated, then crossed to the table. He laid his last dollar on the oilcloth covering.

'High card,' he said.

The gambler moved his eyes to Jubal's stubbled face. For a moment he studied the hard, tough features.

'Seems like I know you stranger . . . a few years back, maybe?' he queried.

'Could be . . . if you've been where I've been,' Jubal answered facetiously.

The gambler gave Jubal another quick look. He shrugged uneasily, set out the deck.

Jubal set his roll down between his worn, cracked boots. He put out a big brown hand and fingered the deck. His fingers merely touched the edges, then he shuffled awkwardly, set the deck down and waited. The gambler sniffed and cut the eight of clubs. Jubal's hand moved out, and without seeming to hesitate he flipped over a red king.

The gambler looked up quickly into Jubal's face, but laid a silver dollar beside the first one.

'You win,' he said with a flat voice.

'Cut again,' Jubal suggested, and smiled thinly.

With his one hand, the gambler riffled the cards. He snapped down the deck and followed the movement of Jubal's hand as he cut.

Jubal laid another red king face up on the table and the smile returned. The gambler hesitated, his hand on the deck. He tapped his fingers restlessly on the top card, then he cut the five of clubs.

The gambler laid two more silver dollars beside

the two in front of Jubal. His eyes moved restlessly.

'We'll have a clean deck, friend,' he said, and reached under the table.

'I didn't ask for one.' Jubal's voice was quick and hard, stopping the movement. 'Leave 'em lay. There's somethin' honest about a dirty deck ... like a farmer's hands.'

The gambler's eyes moved involuntarily to Jubal's own hands.

'You certain we ain't met somewhere?' he asked, an uncertain edge to his voice. 'I'm thinkin' of a time when you likely had less of a hide.' Then he looked towards the bar.

Jubal caught the movement and his thin smile vanished. 'Right this moment, I ain't tryin' too hard to remember,' he said.

The bartender made a sign and the gambler shrugged. A chair scraped and a man came to stand behind Jubal – not too close.

'Mind if I watch?' he asked.

Without looking around, Jubal shook his head; his attention was with the gambler.

'My turn to rearrange them cards,' he said. 'Twice beats the odds. Three times needs a lot a luck. Let's try it, gamblin' man.'

After the fourth cut, the gambler wiped the beaded sweat from his forehead. There were sixteen dollars lying on the checkered oilcloth. A card-table behind Jubal stood empty now, and the men who'd been playing poker stood around watching, some grinning.

The men moved from behind Jubal and he turned to face an older, heavy-set man who stepped forward.

'You've had your fun, mister,' he said. 'Now I'm closin' the game.'

A man behind Jubal interrupted. 'What the hell, Moose. Since when do you close down a little ol' game of cards?'

'When I can't afford to lose any more . . . that's when.' The man looked sharply at the gambler. 'Get some air, Rosey. You look like you need it.'

The gambler pushed himself away from the table. He got to his feet and still mopping at his forehead took another penetrating look at Jubal.

Jubal looked at the money on the table. 'I've worked harder for a lot less than this,' he said, scooping up the two piles of coin.

'Join me for a drink?' the man suggested. 'You keep your money.'

Jubal glanced sideways at him. The man stared back. His face was open, honest-looking.

In his blunt, customary manner, Jubal said, 'No thanks, I got what I came for.'

'One drink . . . you owe me that.' The man smiled.

Jubal looked keenly at the bartender. 'I ain't tasted good whiskey for a long time,' he said.

The man nodded, and the bartender reached under the bar for a bottle of double-rectified.

'I'm Moose Doogle,' the man said. 'This is my saloon.'

Jubal looked around him. 'You own a lot o' this town.'

Doogle studied the end of a fat cigar. 'I own some. But it ain't for a rich return, if that's what you're thinkin'.'

Jubal stood at the bar, watched his whiskey being poured. 'I take your money an' you stand me a drink. Why?' he asked.

Doogle poured his own drink. 'I'm lookin' for someone.'

'You're lookin' for me?'

'Maybe. I ain't lookin' for a greenhorn or fancy Eastern salesman, an' you sure as hell don't look like either.'

Jubal almost smiled, sniffed his drink. 'What do you want of this "someone"? How do I figure?'

'I like the way you handle yourself . . . assessin' the odds . . . quittin' before your luck runs out.'

Jubal thought for a second or two, didn't rise to the implication. 'My luck ran out a long time ago, Mr Doogle. If you're offerin' me somethin', offer it.'

Jubal swallowed his whiskey in one shot and Doogle poured another. Jubal shook his head, pushed the full glass away.

'Temperate too. I like that,' Doogle commented.

'Not necessarily. It's just that one more, an' I *will* owe you, Mr Doogle.'

Jubal picked up his blanket-roll and tugged at the brim of his wolsey hat. 'The card player. You called him Rosey?'

'Yeah, Rosey Mangle. Why?'

'Ask him if he remembers a sodbuster called Birch. Jubal Birch. Had a wife an' kid . . . a piece a land up in Oregon.'

Doogle looked a little interested. 'Stay an' listen to my offer, an' you can ask him yourself.'

Jubal stood very still. He looked down at his pared boots. Out of the corner of his eye he saw the dog. It was lying flat on the boardwalk, its nose under the batwing doors. Its yellow eyes had followed him from the moment he'd entered the saloon.

With a shake of his head, Jubal looked at Doogle. He walked to the card-table, turned his back on the other customers and sat down. 'Get the corn,' he said, with conviction.

Doogle collected the bottle of whiskey from the bartender and followed Jubal to the table.

'I think you *are* the man I'm lookin' for,' he said as he sat down. 'I also think you're Jubal Birch, an' you know Oregon. How'm I doin'?'

Jubal didn't answer the assumption. 'The job an' the pay. Tell me,' he said.

'Takin' a wagon party to Powder River country.'

Jubal looked surprised. Saloon owners don't normally head up wagon trains. 'What's your interest in takin' a party of settlers hundreds of miles north?'

Doogle gave a short laugh. 'Civic duty. Then there's profit from supplies.'

'I guess you own the chandlers too.'

'Lawful activities . . . just ain't that profitable, Mr Birch. That is your name . . . Jubal Birch?' Doogle asked.

Jubal ran his thumb around the top of his glass.

'My name's Jubal Oake,' he said, after a moment's hesitation. 'I just ain't used to usin' it. The places I been, a man's name's just about the last thing you discover about him.'

'Yeah, I understand. A lot of things have changed, Mr Oake. Hopeful folk hit a town, an' the law follows 'em. Cobre Wells ain't changed much in twenty, thirty years. But it will. I heard that in Utah, there's some towns where it's a civil offence to carry a gun in the street.'

'It's been a few years since I was in Utah,' Jubal said.

Doogle eyed him with interest, then continued. 'Most o' the progress is up north. The Northern Pacific's makin' its way across Washington State. The

The Landbreakers

government's made a promise, an' they're settin' up land offices. Any land that folk settle on will be recognized, lawful and proper. If they make an honest go of it an' register, the title's made over.'

Jubal stared doubtfully at Doogle. 'For their sakes, let's hope you're right. Was a time when it was only guns that made things lawful.'

Doogle topped up Jubal's glass, gave a wry smile. 'These people are lumberheaded. They'll make it, if they stick together. The railroad'll run a two-hundred mile spur, for anyone who can guarantee a big enough turnover in supplies. That'll bring in all kinds of business. There'll be telegraph an' press offices . . . an' that's protection.'

Jubal made an understanding smirk. 'That'll be your interest . . . the supply?'

'That's the business I'm in. Think about it. Great Oaks from little acorns. . . ?' Doogle raised his glass, winked at the contrived pun.

But Jubal *was* thinking about it, as he had done seventeen years ago, when he'd set out from Salt Lake City, with Margie and Willum. He sat chewing his lip, listening to the eagerness of Moose Doogle.

'Elko grew from just one man an' a bag a nails. Now it's a real bustlin' town, an' they're runnin' the railroad all the way to Frisco.' Doogle's eyes grew bright. 'There's near a hundred settlers, Mr Oake. They're all good, honest folk, willin' to stake everything on a new way of life. They'll build a fine new town. In ten years there'll be fortunes made.'

Good, honest folk, willin' to stake everything. The words echoed in Jubal's head, rekindling the contempt he still held for the Oregon cattlemen, the pain of losing his wife, the deep hurt for being forced off his land. He remembered the last time he'd thought about the ten-year fortune.

'I ain't interested in dreams,' he said. 'I woke up from 'em. Why do you want my help? You can get maps. Most of that country's been charted.'

Doogle considered his words. 'Maybe we want that big ol' pistol you're carryin' under your coat. Maybe it's instinct about you.'

Jubal thought about Doogle's reasoning. 'Yeah, maybe. But my "big ol' pistol" ain't much use up against dust storms, quicksands, mosquitoes an' fevers. Ain't much good when you're foragin' for roots an' berries when the meat runs out.' He drained his whiskey, placed the glass carefully on the table. 'Bearin' all this in mind, what pay you offerin'?'

'I'm a business man, Mr Oake. You obviously know what you're talkin' about, so I'll pay you more'n a fair dollar. Assumin' that gun's attached to you, I'll fix you up with a new Winchester, an' some new duds. I'm hopin' that's enough. If I'm wrong, tell me now an' you can ride on.'

Jubal fumbled in his pocket for his tobacco, took his time in making a cigarette.

'Right now, a fair dollar sounds a lot,' he said. 'I can get 'em to the Powder River, but that's where it ends. I won't be obligated after that.'

'You won't be. Just get us there.'

'When you reckon on movin' out? If it ain't soon, you can forget goin' anywhere 'til next spring.'

'We're set to move within a week. I'd like you to meet the council before we leave.'

'We? You said, "we". You figure on makin' this trip, Mr Doogle?'

'Yeah. I told you . . . the North's boomin'.'

'What's this council? I ain't never met one o' them before.'

'Most trains have a council. A few of the older ones. Those that have some idea of what they're after . . . what they're gettin' into. Havin' a meetin' gets 'em involved . . . makes 'em feel better.'

Jubal's eyes dropped to his worn-out clothing. He ruefully scratched his grimed, bearded face.

Doogle responded to Jubal's discomfort.

'Probably take a day to get you cleaned up. We'll have the meeting here . . . noon tomorrow,' he said.

'Yeah. I think maybe I'd like to hear this council's notion of what they're gettin' into.' Almost as an aside, Jubal asked, 'You got a gun, Mr Doogle?'

Doogle laughed.

'Oh yes,' he replied enigmatically.

Doogle rose from the table, accepted that Jubal wasn't a shaking-hands man.

'There's a boarding-house down the street,' he said. 'Maybe you saw it when you came in. Take a room after you get yourself cleaned up. Then buy the Winchester. See Barky at the stable . . . he'll pick you out a good horse. Get what else you need, an' put it on my account.'

Jubal looked around for his bedroll and slicker, saw the hound still watching him.

'I haven't yet said I'm goin' to Oregon, Mr Doogle.'

'You will, Mr Oake . . . you will.'

As Jubal left the saloon the clock behind the bar started chiming. It was noon and the first of the day's drinkers pushed past him. They guffawed thirstily and booted aside the dog. It swivelled a wary glance at Jubal, then sloped off to the hardware store.

9
Wagonmaster

'Hey, Wild Bill. My associate here says you musta got lost. Wandered too far from one o' them travellin' shows. Say's that's a real fancy talkin' iron you're carryin'.'

It was early evening, and the muleskinner turned to face Jubal who was standing at the bar. Jubal's beard had been trimmed and he was freshly bathed, newly outfitted at Doogle's expense.

Jubal heard, but paid no attention, sipped his beer. He glanced at the back mirror, saw no sign of Moose Doogle. Mindful of trouble, the bartender pushed a batch of glasses further along the counter.

The muleskinner persisted with his goading. 'Hey, I'm talkin' to you, stranger. Ain't much of a demand for trick shootists in these parts.'

'Leave me be,' Jubal said. 'If you wanna play kids' games, do it in the street.' He pushed a few pennies change along the bar. 'Take this. Go buy some candy.'

'The candy store's closed. I'll just have to have my fun here.' the man grinned offensively. 'Show us a trick with that smoke pole cowboy.' He took a step towards Jubal.

Jubal gritted his teeth, cursed under his breath. He squeezed some of his silver dollars into his fist, pulled his hand clear of his pocket.

'Listen, snake breath,' he hissed. 'There was a time I went unwashed for two years, an' I *never* smelled as bad as you an' if you *ever* had an associate, it would a been a sad an' lonely buffler.'

Good, mature years went into the punch that followed. Jubal's iron-hard fist smashed into the side of the muleskinner's head. He felt the impact wave through his arm, then his chest.

The muleskinner's bulk kept him upright for a few seconds. Then his dull eyes showed that his brain had registered the blow and he went down.

After ten, fifteen seconds Jubal felt the sting in his fingers. He loosed the coin back into his pocket, finished the beer with his left hand.

'I hope that settles it,' he said to the second muleskinner. 'I'm nothin' more'n a man who wants to be left alone . . . wants a quiet drink. Tell your associate that.'

The man on the floor was motionless. He had wild, matted hair, wore a hickory shirt and blanket leggings. A crimson rill dribbled from his ear through the thick, lice-infested whiskers.

Jubal walked away from the bar. He pushed aside one of the batwings and nodded at the dog. Then for a moment he turned back.

'You'll have to smoke-sign it,' he said. 'He'll be deaf, if he ever gets up.'

On the boardwalk, Jubal looked down at the dog. 'We're too good for this place,' he assured it.

Jubal settled for an end-of-town beanery and an early night. He could put aside the incident in the saloon. It had happened many times before – at most points south of the Blue Mountains. He'd grown accustomed to the mark of trouble engraved across his face.

At noon the following day Jubal was standing inside the door of a long, tobacco-filled room above the saloon. He didn't count them, but estimated about fifteen men made up the council. As Doogle had said, they were the 'elders' of the party – mostly middle-aged; they appeared hale and determined.

Doogle started the talk, and he didn't waste much time.

'We got twenty-seven wagons. They're all checked out an' ready to leave within a week. There's thirty-five able men, an' twenty women ... eight youngsters.'

Doogle looked at the men around him who nodded agreement at his estimations.

'Every wagon's gonna be drawn by two mules. We're takin' thirty horses, two hundred longhorns an' there's gonna be some hogs an' chickens. Every wagon's got an inventory of its approximate needs for water an' expendables.'

As Doogle made his way through the schedule, Jubal listened intently. For a saloon owner and businessman, Jubal thought he was doing OK. When he was done with facts and figures, Doogle told the council of his intention to employ Jubal as wagonmaster.

Doogle nodded at Jubal and the men turned to have a look. Other than for acts of defence and hostility, Jubal had always avoided being the focus of attention, and the interest rested uneasily upon him. It was also the first time he'd heard mention of 'wagonmaster' and he wasn't certain it carried the reality.

'Perhaps Mr Oake would like to say a few words to you,' Doogle said.

Jubal walked hesitantly to the side of the room. He looked at each man steadily and searchingly. When he spoke his voice was quiet and controlled, but it held sway.

'What you need to know about me, you'll find out if we make the trip together. I've told Mr Doogle I know the way, an' I can get you there. If you're set on that, you'll make it . . . we all will. But if you're not, then don't even leave town.

'You won't all like what I've got to say, but my words'll hurt a lot less than most other stuff you'll encounter. If you accept me, you accept. . . .'

One or two of the council looked at each other, muttered a few low words. Jubal let them, before he continued.

'Get it in your heads . . . tell your women an' children that we ain't headed for a picnic. At best you'll get ill, an' some'll want to turn back. At worst, some of you won't make it . . . you'll die. You'll spend half your time fightin' for survival and the rest of it recoverin'. I can't even guarantee it'll be worth it when we get there.'

Jubal shot a moot glance at Doogle. 'But Mr Doogle assures me you'll build a fine new town an' make a fortune . . . make everything worth it.'

The council members nodded. They were satisfied in their shared faith, so Jubal pushed his conditions.

'A few miles out of Cobre Wells, you'll find there's a new kinda law enforcement. You men all know the more laws you got, the more they tend to get broke. So we'll have one simple one. Mine.'

The complacent expressions disappeared from the council members' faces. One of them raised his hand, finger pointing.

'See here. . . .' he started.

Jubal looked around the room, stared the man quiet.

'Look at it another way then. If you're uncertain, there'll be no law . . . an' we don't want uncertainty. If any of you men have an argument with that, make it now.'

The man who'd raised his hand said pompously, 'Put like that, we see your point, Mr Oake. After all, we can't expect you to take all the responsibility, with no proper authority.'

'You don't fully understand,' Jubal replied. 'I'll get as many of you as I can to the Powder River, but I ain't wet nursin' on route. You'll do it my way. Any one of you that thinks otherwise could jeopardize lives . . . mine included. I told you already, it ain't gonna be a picnic, an' you better believe it.'

Another man spoke up this time. 'What're you tellin' us, Mr Oake? It sounds like slave-driving.'

Jubal looked at the man thoughtfully. 'Things'll happen, mister, an' we'll have to deal with 'em. Most o' the time you'll be able to handle it between you . . . but sometimes it'll need more than talk an' gentle encouragement. That's where I come in . . . what I'm bein' paid for.'

The Landbreakers

'You mean gun-enforcement, Mr Oake.'

Jubal nodded briefly. 'Try a journey without, an' see what happens. What's your trade, mister?' he asked the man.

'Leatherwork. Had my own store in Pocatello.'

Jubal gave a small, impatient smile. 'Pocatello, huh. Well, if I need some boots repairin', I'll come to you,' he snapped.

'There's no need for ill temper, Mr Oake,' the pompous man said. 'Seems to me you'll be needing a calm and collected behaviour.'

'And how'd *you* earn your money?' Jubal queried the man.

'My name's Gane. Before I decided to make this journey, I was the manager of the Idaho Falls Bank in Idaho Falls.'

'And when I want advice on investin', Mr Gane, I'll be tuggin' at your tent flap.' Jubal looked around the room. 'Do you get my meanin', gentlemen?' he asked, not waiting for an answer. 'Once we get beyond the Owyhee there ain't gonna be any town comforts. It'll be tougher ... more severe than any of you imagined. You'll be facin' thunderstorms, dust-storms an' high rivers. Then there'll be a lack o' water, prairie fires an' grasshopper plagues. Your companions'll be ready to bone an' roll each other.'

Jubal let the detail of his words sink in, then he spoke again. 'You've got some idea of how I'll handle that. If you accept, I'll take the job. If you don't, find someone else,' was his proposition.

Moose Doogle got to his feet, waved his hand at the council.

'Mr Oake's tellin' you how it is ... how it will be. There's none of us here would want it any other way.

We just hadn't been prepared for anyone quite so . . . uncompromising.'

The council members looked suitably thoughtful, and Doogle turned to Jubal.

'If you could give us a short while, Mr Oake, we'll sort this out.'

Jubal appeared to be unconcerned. 'I never move on before sundown,' he said. 'You've got until then. For a while I'll be downstairs . . . in the bar.'

He stepped on to a balcony that fronted the saloon and heard raised agitated voices as he went down the wooden steps. Below him he saw the dog. It looked up, flicked the last few inches of its tail.

Jubal made his way straight to the bar and called for a beer. The bartender had a quick calculating look at the other customers and served him.

'Won't find me makin' comment on that big Colt,' he said, grinning. 'No *sir*!'

Jubal gave him the nearest thing he could get to an amiable smile. For safety he concentrated, watched for the unexpected. After ten minutes, Doogle appeared on the stairs at the end of the barroom and moved his head to indicate the upstairs room. Jubal took another two minutes to drain his glass. He wanted to hear the jaunty, one o'clock chime from the clock above the bar.

The council was in a curious, restless mood. They looked warily at Jubal as he stepped into the room.

Doogle looked more confident. 'It's been decided with a little persuadin' that your case for discipline is befitting the role of wagonmaster . . . bearing in mind the circumstances.'

'Let's hope you don't regret it,' Jubal muttered to himself.

Moose Doogle had started to write something on a piece of paper. Jubal guessed it was probably a last-minute inventory.

'Something to add to your list, Mr Doogle,' he said.

'Yeah, whatever you want,' Doogle replied. He moved close up to Jubal, said quietly. 'Get a table . . . I'll find somethin' suitable. An' I was thinkin' maybe, *Jubal* instead of Mr Oake?'

Jubal watched the council members as they started for the outside steps. He looked thoughtfully at Doogle.

'It was near Powder River that I last heard my first name.'

Doogle started to say something, but Jubal stopped him. 'But that was a long time ago,' he added.

In company with another bottle of labelled whiskey, Jubal gave Doogle his list of wants.

'As well as all that, we need a proofed stock-wagon an' driver. Two kegs o' black powder, an' for every person that carries a gun, fifty rounds of ammunition.'

Doogle raised an eyebrow at the demand, but said, 'I'll see it's done.' He scribbled busily, but this time Jubal reckoned he was worrying about *loss* of profit.

Doogle looked up. 'You think we oughta be takin' a doctor with us, Jubal?' he asked.

Jubal thought, shook his head.

'Aint much a pill-roller can do for cholera when it strikes. For anythin' else . . . nothin' that a good dose a salt an' water won't cure.'

Surprised, and with appropriate concern, Doogle stopped writing for a moment.

'One other thing,' Jubal said. 'You know the men ... maybe most of 'em. Find two that are reliable, even smart. Get 'em to meet me here, about eight tonight. I'll discuss the route with 'em. If you've any maps of the territory, bring 'em.'

'You already thinkin' of the trail, Jubal?'

'More like thinkin' of the ones to avoid.' Jubal looked up and down the street. 'I'll see you here later on,' he said. 'I'm gonna get me some sleep, then a wagonmaster's supper. Me an' that dog that's taken to followin' me around.'

'What's a wagonmaster's supper?' Doogle asked, looking confused.

'A bottle o' whiskey, six eggs, an' a big steak.'

'What you wanna take that mangey cur to supper for?'

'He can eat the steak an' eggs.'

Doogle laughed, and, for maybe the second time in ten years, a smile appeared on Jubal's face.

10
The Ground Rules

An hour after sun-up, the wagons gathered on the outskirts of Cobre Wells. The train stretched in a loose line beyond the corrals and freighter pens. Each canvas-topped wagon was a home in itself. Some of them carried a full family of four or five, one of them eight. There were a few wagon carts – less well appointed and driven by younger, single men.

Jubal nudged his horse slowly along the winding column. He was looking for problems, his eyes missing nothing that was outside of the wagons. As he rode, he couldn't stop his mind straying back to Salt Lake City all those years ago.

After a few minutes he stopped by one wagon. He dismounted and looked closely at a mule with a gush nose. He looked up at the driver.

'You can take that mule out, fella,' he said. 'It ain't sound enough to make the journey.'

'It'll get us to where we're goin', Mr Oake. Little sniffle, that's all.'

'It's strangles, an' it's contagious. That animal won't make it to suppertime. Get it out of line, away from the other animals. Get yourself another ... check it over.'

The driver started to protest, but saw the look in Jubal's face, remembered the council members' warning about Jubal Oake. The man climbed down from his wagon seat and muttered to someone inside. He pulled out a skin pouch, considered the coin it held and tucked it back inside his coat.

'I'm goin' into town,' he called out. 'Pinko, get out here an' unhitch that mule. Take it out a ways an' shoot it. Don't argue, just do it.'

Jubal nodded his approval and moved on.

Further down the line, he stopped again. Without dismounting he looked down at the feet of another mule. 'Your mule's hoof?' he simply queried of the wagon-driver.

'Yes, Mr Oake, we know about it,' said the woman sitting next to the driver. 'It's sandcrack. It can be repaired ... we were told.'

'Take it to the blacksmith, ma'am. Ask him to put a nail through ... a rivet. Ain't too serious, but you'll need to be back within the hour.' Jubal looked at the driver. 'Anythin' else you know about that ain't been tended to?' he asked dryly.

'I don't think so,' the man replied.

'Well, that's all right then,' Jubal mocked as he moved along.

There were other delays, mostly involving livestock or grain for the mules. It was near eight o'clock before the wagons were ready to move off.

Sam Kettle and Big Carrow were the two dependable men Jubal had spoken to earlier about routes, and he sent them ahead as scouts, pathfinders. He'd agreed to talk with the council members each evening before supper to review their headway.

Moose Doogle walked his bay mare near to Jubal. At the head of the train, they looked back along the column of white, canvas-topped wagons. With a sudden thought, Jubal looked about him for the dog, then he nodded at Doogle.

Doogle swung his hat around in a wide arc, and with a sense of moment shouted, 'Let's go.' The journey to Powder River had started.

Eager drivers flicked their whips, jiggled the reins. As wheels creaked in their first rolling movement, they called encouragement to their mule teams. Within ten minutes the wagon train picked up, began to snake its way to the north-west.

Out on the flank two riders whooped noisily at the cattle. The milling herd broke, then stretched forward into a steady, brawny walk.

Doogle whistled through his teeth and called out to Jubal. 'Can you hear it?'

The two men sat their horses, silent for a while. The crisp morning air was filled with the chaotic sound of creaking and groaning wagons, lowing cattle and yapping dogs.

'It's the sounds of life rollin' into a new world.'

Jubal looked at him sideways, then up at the vast blue sky. He pulled down the brim of his Stetson and didn't respond.

Milo Milk galloped his horse to the head of the train. He pulled in and slowed to a walk alongside Moose Doogle's wagon.

'Look at that, Mr Doogle. All these men an' women . . . childer an' all. It's gonna be a real party, Mr Doogle,' he said excitedly.

'How old are you?' Jubal called across to him.

'Fourteen next birthday, sir.'

'Don't throw away your old boots, boy. Not until you get new ones.'

With that, Jubal gigged his horse. He took up point, a few hundred yards ahead of the train. For a while his face revealed the grief of recollection.

Young Milo looked enquiringly at Doogle. 'What's he mean, Mr Doogle?'

Doogle shrugged. 'Somethin' to do with *prospect*, I think. But don't ask him, kid . . . don't ever ask him.'

'My pa says he don't speak civil to no one, Mr Doogle.'

'Your pa's right, kid, but he don't know why.'

Doogle turned his horse. As he rode back along the line of wagons he realized he didn't know why, either.

With sound wagons and fresh, healthy animals the train made good passage – nearly eighty miles in the first few days.

As they moved west, then north, the land slowly changed. The plains became more undulating – ridges of distant shadow indicated their closeness to the Sawtooths. The grass became more abundant, grew richer and the cattle took to a mid-morning graze.

At night camp, the mules and horses were hobbled and blankets spread. Fires of brushwood and dry dung were lighted, and folk sat around eating dumplings and roasted meats. Stars of familiar constellations hung in the big sky, and the migrants talked excitedly of the future. Some of them sang songs, played musical instruments, even danced.

Jubal took no part in genial, social activity. He

confined himself to the stock-wagon. After his nightly meetings with Sam Kettle, Big Carrow and the council he sat quietly making cigarettes, turning cards, occasionally thinking. He was a man alone, not seeking or needing the company of others. It was only when they broke camp in the early mornings that he moved among them – checking the wagons, mindful of potential trouble.

On the fifth day out, a council member reported to Jubal that one of the wagons had broken a wheel. Jubal turned and cantered back down the line.

The wagon was almost pitched on its side. One of the large rear wheels was shattered and half its spokes were broken. For a short distance, the wheel hub had ploughed through the ground, the strain wrenching disastrously at the braces and rear axle.

Jubal had a quick look and growled at the driver.

'The ground's good . . . what the hell you carryin' in that wagon, mister?'

The man mumbled something, and Jubal leaned forward.

'What you sayin'?' he shouted, as the man's wife and child appeared from behind the wagon.

'Musta been faulty all the time, an' I ain't carryin' a spare.'

Jubal turned to the man who'd told him of the breakdown.

'What's your name?' he asked.

'Cove Booker.'

'Get half a dozen men. Booker. Take the good wheels an' tie 'em in under some of the lighter wagons. Hitch the mules behind the stock-wagon.' Jubal turned to the driver. 'If you can find anyone that's willin', you can share out the things you want to keep. Leave the rest.'

'There's no need for any of that, Mr Oake. With a bit of help, I can repair that wheel in a few hours.'

Jubal swore silently. 'You brought along a faulty wagon, an' now you're leavin' it. Unless you reckon on stakin' a claim out here, you'll be findin' bed-ground in some o' the other wagons.

'Find bed-ground, be damned. Apart from a busted wheel this is a fine, solid wagon, an' I ain't leavin' it here.' The driver was irked at Jubal's severity.

Jubal shook his head, sat chafing as Moose Doogle rode up. He was with Booker, who returned with three other men.

'What's happened here?' Doogle asked, needlessly.

'What's it look like,' Jubal snapped. 'You men, get those wheels off . . . best unload first.

Doogle considered the situation, saw there was no chance of the wagon continuing. He looked at Jubal then quickly rode off.

From beside the broken-down wagon, the driver looked up at Jubal.

'I can make the repairs an' catch you up sometime tomorrow.' The man stood his ground, stubbornly. 'I ain't takin' this soft o' stuff from you Mr Oake,' he said.

Jubal just looked. Pig-headed an' very, very stupid, he thought to himself. He nodded at the men, and two of them started to off-load the wagon. Booker and the other men checked over the three good wheels.

Dressed in plain homespuns, the man's wife and daughter stood back. Tightly clasping the little girl's shoulders, his wife was quiet and miserable.

The driver looked at Jubal, then at the men unloading the family's chattels. His hand moved towards a small Colt he carried high and tight around his waist.

Jubal saw the threat, tut-tutted.

'Your wagon ain't goin' anywhere an' these men ain't got time to dig a hole,' he said flatly. 'Don't be a chancer all your life.'

Booker grabbed at one of the front wheels and gave it a firm tug. He glanced shifty and heedful at his colleague.

For fifteen minutes the man watched as his family's personal belongings were shared around the last of the wagons as they passed by.

'That wagon cost me an' mine just about everythin',' he said.

Jubal knew, but sat his horse in silence.

At last there was nothing left, other than a wooden chest and a small bookcase. Stripped of its wheels and canvas awning, the wagon became a skeletal grave, a marker along the trail.

The man stood and watched until Jubal told him to take one of the rear wagons.

For a moment the man stared at him, his hands hanging useless at his sides. Jubal waited until he'd spoken to the driver of the last but one wagon and climbed reluctantly aboard. The man sat on the lowered tail-gate, and Jubal understood the frustration and anger that distorted the man's face.

Five minutes later Jubal nodded at the driver of the stock-wagon. Because of its cargo it was well to the rear of the train. The driver indicated with his thumb that Jubal should look back along the trail.

About a half-mile distant, he saw the hound from Cobre Wells. It was following, taking a zigzag course, pursuing the trail and Jubal Oake.

When Jubal eventually returned to the head of the train, Doogle said to him: 'I ain't one to interfere, Jubal, but you know three or four men *could*'ve repaired that wagon. Wouldn't have taken more'n three, four hours.'

Jubal said quietly, looking straight ahead: 'You gotta look at the broader picture, Moose. We been on the trail for five days, an' this is the first time we been bothered. But think on it. We got twenty-eight wagons in this train, so pretty soon, there's gonna be a heap more trouble. Most of it'll be the wheels an' axles, an' we ain't even on broken ground yet.'

Doogle listened thoughtfully, as Jubal continued with his explanation.

'We can't hold up every time a wagon breaks down. Right now we got three spare wheels. When we use 'em up – an' we will – the wagon after that'll get left behind . . . just like that one.'

Doogle thought it over.

'Well, they ain't *all* gonna break down, Jubal, but I see what you're drivin' at. But is it *that* important for us to save a few hours . . . even a few days?'

'You still ain't considerin' the broader picture,' Jubal said wearily. 'There's twenty-eight wagons. That's a lot a mendin' time for all of 'em . . . must be more'n three days, added up. Even with favourable conditions, it's gonna be tough beyond the state line. But what happens if we're into the basin, betwixt rivers, an' our water's down? Believe me, Moose, there'll be a lot of your "good, honest folk" who'll close their eyes . . . ride round a busted wagon *then*.

That's when those few more hours'll likely mean their own death . . . or their young 'uns'.'

'Them breakdowns ain't likely to happen all at the same time,' Doogle repeated. 'But you know best, Jubal, I'll concede that.'

'Yeah, remember that's what you're payin' me for.'

They rode on a mile or so in silence, before Jubal spoke.

'Mr Doogle,' he said.

'Moose,' Doogle said. 'Make it Moose.'

'Yeah. Let's get straight, Moose. I'm takin' as many of these people as possible to Powder River country. That means doin' it my way, an' *that*'s what I'm bein' paid for.'

Doogle was going to repeat his opinion, his reservations, but thought better of it and kept quiet. Whatever he thought of Jubal Oake's disposition, it was the method of the man that would see them through. Bearing in mind that the journey wasn't for ever, he held up his hand in approval.

11
A Quarrel

It was early evening of the same day that Big Carrow rode back to report of a river ahead. It was the Owyhee, a fork of Snake River, and in full spate. The train had to veer east for two hours before a shallow enough crossing was found. It was after first dark before supper fires were lit and night preparations made.

Early next morning the train had hardly stirred before Jubal was calling for a move. It was almost two hours earlier than previous starts to the day; the ground still held its night-time chill.

That was the start of a shift in the nature of the wagon-train's journey into Oregon. For some reason Jubal had set a new pace – an excessive, killing rate of advance. He'd told Moose Doogle, the drivers and the council to urge the wagons and cattle to greater speed. For many days, Jubal forced the advance. It was a relentless push, even using the morning graze to progress a few more miles. Under the sun for hours on end, the drivers were burning up, their tempers stretched, nerves ragged. In the evenings, quarrels broke out between those who understood and those who didn't. Twice, Moose Doogle had to separate flailing fists before Jubal arrived; drivers who were determined to trade punches because they couldn't settle their differing opinions with words.

Worried about the crack in morale, Cove Booker spoke with Doogle about Jubal's new strategy.

'Don't make a lot a sense, Moose, an' you know it. Speak to Oake, find out what's goin' on.'

'I already have. He reminded me that we all agreed to do it his way. In return he'd get us to the Powder River.'

'That was you an' the council, Moose. Some of the folk reckon it weren't such a good agreement.'

'I'll tell you what I told young Milk. Think long an' careful, if you're gonna put that reckonin' to Oake.'

'I ain't,' Booker returned. 'It's just that a lot a the older ones are gettin' tired, Moose . . . real tired.'

'I know, Cove, but I can't do much about it.'

'Maybe it's Injun country, Moose? He's runnin' us through badlands . . . don't want to frighten us by tellin'.'

'Any Injuns out here, Cove, will be long dead,' Doogle said. He gave a reassuring grip to Cove's shoulder. 'Why don't you try an' calm them folk down a bit . . . those that are worried. Remember, nothin' lasts for ever.

Booker was right about some of the more elderly being tired. Jubal Oake had kept up the grind, and his course for the day had appalled them, pushed some to the limits of their control. During the long day, they'd not rested, eaten only what they'd been able to hash up on the moving wagon, including breakfast.

When they made camp, they'd been driving for nearly fifteen hours. There was no singing or dancing that night – everybody was longing for sleep.

But there was no let-up. Long before daybreak the following morning, tired scowling families were being hectored into movement.

By midday the men had become deeply troubled, dangerously sullen. Jubal could sense the hostility as he rode the check line.

It was during late afternoon that Jubal heard the firing of a rifle somewhere near the end of the line. He swung his horse's head and dug his heels, took a fast canter to find the cause of the shooting.

Someone was pounding shells at small rocks and into gopher holes. The man's aim was good from a driving-seat, but the act of doing it didn't impress Jubal. He reined in his horse, gripped the front canvas hoop.

'What the hell you doin'?' he yelled. 'You tryin' to spook the herd? Put that damn pop-gun away or I'll break it over your thick head.'

The man was solidly built, with broad shoulders, big arms and hands. A straggly moustache made him look older than his years. He held the butt of a .36 Yellowboy against the driving-seat, pointed it at the sky. Then he turned, cool, composed.

'The herd's too far away to be spooked, an' I've just about had it with you . . . Mr Oake,' he said. 'Had it with your fear-makin' an' pushin' us around. If I hadn't put them bullets into gopher holes, I just might've been tempted to put 'em into you . . . Mr Oake.' The man was close to Jubal, spirit showing in his eyes. 'Now, if you don't mind, I'm stoppin' my wagon right here, an' I'm sleepin' 'til noon tomorrow.'

Jubal took off his Stetson, hung it on the horn of his saddle.

'Seems to me you're doin' the pushin',' he replied. 'If it's a fight you're wantin', then I'll oblige. But it ain't a killin' issue, and other than dumpin', it's the only thing I'll stop on the trail for.'

The man placed his Yellowboy and bleached fedora on the seat beside him and climbed down. Jubal dismounted and removed his gun-belt, looped it under the Stetson. The man rolled up his sleeves, Jubal didn't bother.

'I ain't normally too interested in a man who I'm about to put down,' he said. 'But in your case, I'll make an exception. What's your name?'

'Will Hammer,' said the man, simply.

No sooner had the men squared up to each other than wagons pulled to a halt. It was the visceral relief that most of them had been waiting for. Within moments a crowd had gathered; men, and their women and children, forming themselves into a big semicircle around one side of the wagon.

The two men were shifting sideways, warily circling each other as Jubal had intended. Will was holding his hand up against the dipping sun when Jubal moved in, smacked him hard across the mouth.

Will shook his head, wiped a trickle of blood from his split lip. He spat into the ground, and without looking up, lunged suddenly at Jubal. Both men went sprawling in the dust. Jubal was underneath, at a disadvantage, but he'd fought like this before. As both men hit the ground, he was already twisting himself from Will's weight. He rolled on to one knee, drove a short, hard punch into the side of Will's ribs. He heard the sharp intake of breath, and he drove his fist in again. Will's body recoiled, and Jubal edged away, backed off three paces.

Will pushed himself to his feet. His mouth was bloody, and his face was flushed with irrepressible anger.

'That's enough. Get back on your wagon. We'll say no more of it,' Jubal said.

But Will was heated. He clenched his fists, as if in grim defeat, then made another wild lunge at Jubal. Jubal hadn't expected it, and he moved a bit late. He swayed to one side, but Will's raking fist caught him above his eye, snapped his head sideways. He stumbled sideways, and another fist buried itself low in his belly. He grunted with pain, and as he doubled up, Will caught him with a punch that cracked into his jawbone. His legs buckled, and he staggered backwards up against the front wheel of Will's wagon. The pain shocked him, and for a few stunned seconds he stared at the ground between his feet. He took a shallow breath and blinked several times, painfully. When he looked up, he was confused by the blurred silhouette above him. Will was standing with his back to the sun, glaring down.

Jubal reached up a hand and grabbed one of the wheel-spokes. He pulled himself to his feet, sniffed and shook his head.

'Well, Mr Hammer, you've made your point,' he said, clasping his chin. 'Now . . . before I get real angry, climb back on that wagon.'

Will looked around him at the people watching. A few turned away, others smiled self-consciously; some he noticed, were indicating encouragement.

'I just told you, Mr Oake . . . I'm stayin' here 'til tomorrow.' Will was feeling confident, satisfied that he'd put Jubal on the floor. 'You best listen to what I've been tellin' you,' he said.

'I take it that was your best shot, settler?' Jubal spat the words into the soil, then hauled himself up.

He walked straight at Will. He didn't raise his hands, take up any form of guard; he just moved in towards his young opponent. Will piled out a straight arm, again at Jubal's face. Jubal simply flicked his head to one side, felt the knuckles scrape below his ear. Without slowing, he went in on Will.

Jubal wasn't out of control, he just decided to finish what he'd started. Will Hammer should have heeded the wagonmaster's warning. But how was he to know the Jubal Oake didn't ask anybody three times . . . ever.

Will covered up, took the first blows along his forearms. But they were hard and he tried to turn away. A low punch caught him in the kidneys and he gasped, staggered with the flush of pain. He turned back, immediately took Jubal's knuckles deep in his stomach. Jubal hit him again, this time in the side of his face, then the other side, higher near his eye.

Will's face was split and bruised, blood ran into his mouth, down past his chin on to his throat. His eyes were swollen, half-closed, and his leg-joints were jellying beneath him, but he didn't go down.

The watching children were led away by their parents, the women near to tears. One of the men shouted for them to stop, but like many years before, the blood ran hot in Jubal's veins.

Will lurched forward, took a wild swing at Jubal.

Jubal sidestepped him and meted out one of his favourite stoppers. His fist pounded into Will's ear, the impact making Jubal stumble forward as Will fell beside him. Jubal took a pace back; his chest was heaving and he stood biting his lip.

He thought of those watching. He looked around him, but the small crowd had broken up. There was no one there. No one to witness his beating. Then he saw the movement of someone at the back of the wagon. It was Milo Milk, and his young face showed revulsion for what he'd seen.

Jubal wasn't much concerned about Milo Milk's sentiment, or anyone else's. But when he saw Will attempting to rise up at him, he suffered a curious and rare twinge of feeling, and not just for the man's defiance. He ran his fingers through his hair, brushed at the front of his shirt.

'Drive this wagon while you can,' he rasped. 'Any more from me, an' you'll be lyin' in the back.'

Will was swaying on his feet. He sniffed and spat blood, the agony in his head blinding him. Dust was clogging his eyes, and he flailed his arms uselessly, as again he sought out Jubal.

Jubal backed off, avoided a wild, swinging first. He dipped, allowed the punch to break into his shoulder. Then he grabbed Will's arm and twisted him around. He stuck out his foot, caught him low on the shin as he crashed forward, away from him. Will bludgeoned into the side of the wagon, let out a tormented sigh, and collapsed. His shoulders heaved once and he pushed a hand against the ground. But, for Will Hammer, the best part of the day was over. He turned over and lay still.

'Don't know when you're beat,' Jubal said.

Breathing deeply, he stood watching Will for a few moments. Then a strange feeling gripped him, deep inside. He recalled something, a recollection from far off. It was the manner in which Will Hammer was lying motionless on the ground; the sight of the scarred flesh of an ear-lobe.

Jubal threw off the unsettling chimera and turned, called out to the mounted figure behind the rear of the wagon.

'It's over now, kid. You can help him into the wagon when he comes to. Take over the team. Mr Hammer probably won't feel like havin' his bones jostled for a while. Unlike me,' he added with bite.

With his jaw and half his face aching, Jubal went to his horse and climbed stiffly into the saddle. He pulled on his Stetson and buckled on his gun-belt, spurred his horse towards the front of the wagon-train. As he rode the line he imagined more than saw the vengeful faces, the mutterings of unrest. He wondered how much control he'd lost in the last quarter-hour.

He rode a hundred yards ahead of the lead wagon, then slowed as Moose Doogle rode alongside him.

After a minute or so Doogle edged his mare in close and looked across at Jubal.

'I guess you took care o' that sniff o' trouble then,' he suggested.

'Yeah. Nothin' I couldn't handle. Where'd that Will Hammer come from?' Jubal asked, nervous and unsettled.

Doogle shook his head slowly. 'Never said. I know he don't mix much, an' he's a lot younger than he makes out.'

'How old?'

The Landbreakers

'No more'n sixteen, I'd say. Why you interested?'

'Dunno . . . it's just somethin' . . . almost as if he was tryin' to run off them steers . . . stampede 'em on purpose.'

'Nah, he was only havin' a bit a fun . . . wasn't thinkin'. A lot o' these people are tuckered out, Jubal. You don't even meet with the council any more. They won't take much more o' your pushin'.'

'They'll take it. An' out here, funnin' has limits . . . idiocy don't.'

'Don't make the mistake of thinkin' they're idiots, Jubal. Some of 'em are real full o' school learnin'. I told you, they're tired an' proddy. One little snap they don't take to, an' they're off . . . spooked outa control.' Doogle had a quick glance at Jubal. 'That's what happened with Will Hammer. He didn't mean no harm, an' you know it.'

'You reckon he's had some school learnin'?' Jubal asked, trying to disguise his interest.

'I told you, I know nothin' about him. But I'd say, yeah . . . some.'

Jubal returned Doogle's inquisitive look. 'He was pushin' for a fight, Moose. He as good as told me. I gave him a way out.'

'Sure you did Jubal. So obligin' you held the door for him.'

Jubal twisted in the saddle, winced at the pain in his belly.

'The goin's easy at the moment, Moose, but it ain't gonna stay that way. There's unforgivin' land awaitin' us, an' I gotta have control . . . the whip hand. If someone's gonna fight every time. . . .'

Before he finished the sentence, he felt he'd been struck by lighting. The man's name was Will

Hammer, *now*. But years ago it was Willum Birch. The in-between years had dramatically changed his appearance and he'd grown some, but Jubal knew that the young wagon driver he'd beaten to the ground was his son.

Doogle interrupted Jubal's wild thoughts.

'No one's gonna fight every time, Jubal. Why don't you ease up? Never hear of "less whip, more control"?'

'Yeah ... I've heard of it,' Jubal said, his mind suddenly far away. 'You reckon that's appropriate, do you, Moose?'

'Yeah, I do.' Doogle was troubled and worried by Jubal's bullheadedness. 'But I'll continue to do your biddin', if that's what pleases you ... if it keeps me from bein' beaten senseless.'

12
Hard Run

Jubal paid no heed to Moose Doogle's concerns. For another two days he maintained the run, unrelenting in his urge to make way across the basin. It was when the train struck camp early on the morning of the third day that he imposed the next set-back. He decided that from then on all water supplies would have to be conserved; each wagon to spin out a daily ration.

The migrants were all in, downcast and expended from lack of sleep. Now they were being dried out under countless hours of burning sun. There was nowhere to hide, nowhere to escape the heat. Under canvas, children who didn't understand were whimpering from the discomfort.

When, after five days of the gruelling trek, Kettle and Carrow led them to a fork of the Snake River, it needed no ghost to tell Jubal Oake of the wagon train's resentment towards him.

They were incensed for not knowing why they'd been driven relentlessly. Whole families had suffered nearly a week of deprivation, only to end up alongside as much fresh, free-flowing water as they wanted.

Moose Doogle was a little more circumspect, and had guessed otherwise. An hour after the wagons had rolled along the river, he sat his horse, watched Milo Milk and a few other youngsters dangle a hook from a low cutbank. He turned to Jubal.

'You knew of this river?' he asked.

'Yeah, I knew of it,' Jubal answered.

'It runs flat. Looks like maybe it could run dry, this time o' year.'

'Yeah, it runs dry . . . happens overnight,' Jubal said. 'Then again, sometimes the water's so bad, you can chew it. I guess we're just lucky.'

'How long 'til we make the next river?' asked Doogle.

'The John Day? Five, six days, maybe.'

Doogle nodded, thoughtfully. 'That'll be sixteen days from the Owyhee.'

'I would a made it in fifteen.'

'If there'd been nothin' drinkable here . . . that's more'n two weeks between water. We'd a been mighty low by the time we made it to the John Day.'

'That's the way I had it figured,' said Jubal.

Doogle grinned as he understood Jubal's sanction on the water supplies. 'Yeah, I nearly forgot,' he responded. 'You've been this way before.'

Jubal didn't answer, and Doogle looked along the river bank. Milo Milk was hauling out baby catfish, others were collecting dry brush for the cooking-fires.

'Looks like Will Hammer's mended,' Doogle said, in good humour. 'He's a hard one.'

Jubal looked along the line of wagons. 'Yeah,' he

agreed, sounding surprised. 'He ain't even limpin'.'

'No reason why he should, is there? I was told it was his face you spent most time on.'

'Yeah, but he should a felt it down to his feet.'

Doogle whistled through his teeth. 'One day I guess you'll tell me where you got that streak o' tenderness, Jubal.'

'If you happen to get close, tell him he fought good,' Jubal said, disregarding Doogle's sarcasm.

'Somewhere under that rawhide beats a human heart,' Doogle said. 'If you told those folk why you rationed the water . . . they'd understand.'

'I ain't obliged to tell 'em anythin' an' I don't aim to. We're well beyond the point of no return, so they won't be turnin' back 'cause o' my sting.'

Doogle shrugged his shoulders. 'It's your business, Jubal. I think I'll tell Will Hammer you were askin' after him.'

Feeling was still running high, when the wagons rolled again the following day. Just by association with Jubal, Doogle felt some of the settlers' rancour directed at himself.

On the continuing arduous journey hopes and aspirations for the future became more remote. The settlers turned to thinking about the present, how to survive the hostility of the land *and* Jubal Oake.

In the choking dust, the vast land stretched eternally before them. North of the Snake River, a dozen streams and rivers had to be forded or swum. On the edge of the basin, mules had to be urged from quicksands, whipped into dashing torrents or hauled up muddy banks. At night, the train arrived parched or drenched at the evening camp. It was the settlers' only relaxation, but they fell asleep to the howl of marauding wolves, under the vicious hum of thick mosquito-clouds.

In the chill early mornings, the weariness started once more, as the train wended its way to a destination still too distant for the migrants to reflect on. They had reached a point of hardly seeing, hardly thinking. None of them saw the thin, distant plume of smoke that rose from the floor of the treeless plain. Nor did they consider the unbroken vigilance of the man they vented their torment on.

Jubal reined in his horse. He sat very still, watching the smoke as it curled into the blue Oregon sky. He waited patiently for Kettle and Carrow to ride back from their advance scouting.

'You seen it, Jubal? We didn't get that close. Thought it best we ride back,' Carrow yelled, as the two scouts swung their horses either side of Jubal.

'What you reckon's out there?' Kettle asked.

Jubal answered slowly. 'Shapeleels is one word for 'em. They'll be Modoc or Chinook.'

'What do they want?' Carrow wanted to know.

Jubal squinted against the high sun. 'Ride back an' ask 'em,' he said.

'I didn't know there were hostiles out here, any more.' Kettle sounded uncertain.

'There ain't. The army took care of that. They'll keep their distance . . . ride around us . . . pick up what we're gonna leave behind.'

'What's that?' Carrow asked.

'A box o' coloured beads, hand-mirrors an' some bags o' Bull Durham. We'll stash it all under a dozen wool blankets.'

'Where we gonna get that stuff from?' Kettle asked puzzled.

'The stock-wagon. I got all that an' more loaded up in Cobre Wells. Thought it might come in handy.'

Carrow looked doubtfully at Jubal. 'What do you want we should do?'

'Get Moose Doogle an' Cove Booker. Tell 'em what's happenin'. Then ride the wagon line. Make sure all those that got guns know how to load an' use 'em.'

'Where you goin'?' Kettle wanted to know.

'I'm gonna ride out . . . take a looksee. If they're Chinook, we'll leave a case of whiskey.'

'Why'd we want to waste good whiskey on Injuns?'

'It ain't good whiskey, an' it won't be wasted. If they're Chinook, we're in trouble. But with the drink inside 'em, they'll stay roostered for two or three days. By then, we'll be moving through the foothills of the Blue Mountains.'

That evening Jubal ordered the small herd to be moved in close, and the wagons to form a circle. He'd discovered the Indians were Chinooks, and he wasn't taking any chances. He didn't think the renegades would attack the train before first light. But by then they'd have headed out and the drink would be there for the finding.

By the light from a camp-fire, he made up the stash of gifts. He added a few more gaudy trifles, things to keep the Indians occupied while they made themselves sick on Moose Doogle's bug-juice.

Beneath the stock-wagon the chasing dog pressed its jowls into the parched soil. Jubal heard the low growl, saw its eyes reflecting yellow in the glow from the fire.

13
The Full Circle

Ten days later the wagon-train was noon-camped in a lush green valley. The soil was good, the land protected in a vast, tree-lined curve of the Powder River. After a short meeting, the council decided they were near to the end of their journey.

'This is as far as you need take us,' said Moose Doogle to Jubal Oake. 'We can make our separate ways along the valley. Some of us are more obliged than others, but you ain't bein' paid on the difference.'

Jubal removed his hat, slapped it against his leg.

'You carryin' my money on you?' he asked.

Doogle shook his head. 'No. In a couple o' days I'm riding to Bakerville. It can't be more than a day's ride. I've got business to sort out. Come with me, an' I'll draw your money from the cattlemen's bank.'

Jubal replaced his hat, scratched his beard. He remembered Bakerville from many years ago. It was where he'd gone to trade. Where he'd bought candy and a clasp-knife for Willum, a mail-catalogue for Margie.

'I know Bakerville,' he said. 'Don't recall it havin' a bank.'

That evening while the new settlers enjoyed a weary celebration, the two men sat talking beside Doogle's store-wagon.

'Have you thought about where you'll be headed next?' Doogle asked Jubal.

'Nope. Not so certain as I'll be headed anywhere,' Jubal answered. 'Like you, I've business to sort out.'

Doogle looked warily at Jubal. 'You ain't in business, Jubal, an' it ain't rightly any o' mine, but. . . .'

'But you're gonna ask anyway,' Jubal interrupted.

'Why not? We're not goin' anywhere.' Doogle handed over a tin mug that held an inch of brand whiskey. 'This business,' he said. 'It's to do with somethin' that happened a long time ago. An' I'm guessin' it's the reason you accepted my offer of a job . . . gave you a purpose for comin' back.'

'You carry on with your guessin' Moose, but the truth is, time's wearin' away at me. Maybe I will stake out some land an' settle right here.'

Doogle chuckled. 'Well I ain't your lawyer or your doctor, so you're not obliged to tell me the truth.' Doogle poured another smack of whiskey. 'If you do picket a section, Jubal, I can register it. We're all gonna get title . . . government deeds to say it's legally our land.'

Jubal drained his mug, got to his feet.

'Thanks for the drink, Moose. Settles the trail dust,' he said. 'No need for you to register anythin' I choose to make mine. A piece o' paper's never stopped anyone takin' land if they've a mind to.'

'Times have changed, Jubal. Deeds makes things

legal. Now there's government offices to approve an' sanction,' Doogle advised.

Jubal shook his head, tossed his empty mug at Doogle.

'Nope,' he said. 'Times might a changed, but I haven't.'

But Jubal Oake had to face up to his years of hurt and wretchedness. In the shadow of the Blue Mountains, his life seemed to have gone full circle, and with the coming of Will Hammer, fate had taken a hand. Perhaps Moose Doogle was right, he thought. Perhaps, within a major settlement along the Powder River, he wouldn't have to fight cowmen from his land. Perhaps, he could start afresh.

But the old wounds ran deep. Jubal would never forget those who forced him from his land, took the life of his wife. He wasn't going to ride away again from his own son. The pain of Strawberry Creek had gnawed in his gut for ten years. He'd pondered on Willum's new, adopted name of Will Hammer. William had been his christened name, but he'd have made Hammer out of Hamerdal – the good Norwegians who'd looked after him, given him the schooling.

Jubal wondered if Will had sensed anything, as he himself had done during their recent fist fight. He wanted to explain, let Will know that he was his father, but he couldn't. He knew he could never find the words, make any compensation, for the lost years. There was no doubt of the loathing that Will would have harboured for Jubal Birch; the father who'd deserted him as a child, who was blameable for the death of his mother.

There had been one occasion when Jubal had spoken to Will. He'd tried to tell him there was no animosity or hard feelings from their nonsensical brawl, to hang out a clue to their kinship. But there was no quarter from Will. He heard Jubal out in silence, then turned away indifferently – returned to his new life in company with the settlers from Utah.

A few miles upriver from the main settlement, and in due time, Jubal had taken Doogle's advice. He'd staked out a small piece of land, and with money earned from bringing the wagons in safely, he'd employed a few men to build him a modest dwelling and outbuildings.

At the eastern end of the settlement, where the river started to bend, a lone stand of yellow pine jutted from the line of willows that bordered the river. It was an obvious landmark, and as such gave its name to the new township.

Using the Overland Mail from Bakerville, then the telegraph from Boise and Twin Falls, Moose Doogle had engaged land and property agents. He decided to sell all his interests in Cobre Wells. For the immediate future, he'd remain in Yellow Pine carving out new business ventures, trying again for his elusive fortune.

The settlers worked hard from the moment they arrived in Powder River country. They inspanned mules and ploughed the first furrows, sowed wheat, maize and vegetables. It was the wrong time of year though, and all the first crops died. But they persisted, and as the months passed, Yellow Pine grew into a small town. At the start, the buildings were rough-planked with canvas walls, embellished

The Landbreakers

with false fronts. Then some merchants added another storey, others put up awnings, built raised sidewalks.

The community of settlers rekindled their trades; carpenters, corn-chandlers, carters, a blacksmith, even a barber. Moose Doogle opened a livery stable and a store that stocked everything that might be needed. Farm machinery and guns, ground coffee, 'air-tights' of peaches and tomatoes, spices, rolls of bright-coloured cloth and bonnets for the ladies. In the third year a telegraph operator opened an office, and a regular mail service was in operation. Doogle also built his saloon; he called it Trail's End. After five years the Northern Pacific drove a rail spur south from Spokane. From Bakerville, Yellow Pine now had a trade link that stretched from Seattle in the west to the Great Lakes in the east.

In those years, with Moose Doogle at the helm, Yellow Pine grew and got prosperous. In the rich Oregon soil, the crop yield was choice and abundant. From a breed stock of Poll Durhams, small herds of grade cattle dotted the pasture land along the Powder River. From fewer than seventy original settlers, the immigrant community had grown to nearly four hundred.

But, like all the emerging, prosperous towns of the new West, it was considered an open shoot for any gunmen, gamblers and hell-raisers. Hugger-muggered with a bank, doctor's surgery and stage-office, saloon girls and faro tables vied to separate the naive townsfolk from their hard-earned money. Mugsful of rough, cheap liquor, served to farmers and trail drifters alike, provoked reckless behaviour. The resulting gun-play often created lethal entertainment for bystanders; then trade for an undertaker, another hole in Yellow Pine's bone-orchard.

The original council that had been formed in Cobre Wells when the settlers decided to set out for Oregon, still held regular meetings. With Moose Doogle as leader, the group advised on business and developments for the town.

But progress brought its troubles, and in the fast-changing times, Doogle was one of the first to realize the danger that was embracing Yellow Pine; the breakdown of order, the cramp of lawlessness. Consequently, the town council sought and nominated a reliable and determined man for its citizens to elect as sheriff.

Will Hammer found the job of sheriff rewarding, but it was hard work. From the outset, he deputized Sam Kettle and Big Carrow to check riotous conduct and to try and keep gunfights off the streets. But with diligence and the frequent laying-on of gun-barrel and fists, law and order was gradually imposed. For Will Hammer, the ability to mete out rough and ready justice came as second nature, like an inherited feature. As a peace officer, he turned from any fair fight, but he dealt harshly with wanton, unjust killing, mob rule and the customary horse-thieving.

As time passed, and the law established itself, Yellow Pine began to attract a different sort of trouble. There were four-flushers and finance cheats attracted by the thriving community and scope for quick and easy profit. Margin purchasers rooked innocent folk by double-dealing; a business that once would have been robbery by intimidation and bullets.

During this time Jubal kept his head down. He

lived a peaceable, almost reclusive life, and his needs were modest. He appeared to be content with tending his parcel of land, occasionally playing a game of cards in Moose Doogle's Trail's End Saloon. But only Jubal knew it was a cover for what he was really doing. He was close to Will Hammer, living out his own life through his son's. Watching Will carry out his duties as sheriff gave him an inner pride, healed some of the bitterness he'd always felt since the death of his wife.

But Jubal was far from happy. The life of a farmer had never meant anything after his downfall at Strawberry Creek, but nobody in Yellow Pine knew of that. At a time and place where reputations lasted only as long as it took a body to hit the ground, only a few remembered that it was Jubal Oake who brought them from Cobre Wells. But a few heard tell of the tale.

Once in a while, Jubal would talk with Moose Doogle, steer the conversation round to the sheriff and his doings. He saw Will, but he never spoke. Will would nod to him from his office across the street, but it was a cursory, formal recognition, nothing more. Jubal thought it must be more than the fist fight that created the vital barrier between them. The torment was almost more than anything he'd ever experienced.

14
The Land Offer

One evening late in the Fall, Jubal was sitting on the sidewalk outside the Trail's End. He was alone, mulling on the day, when a man wearing a cheap worn suit stepped up alongside his bench. He didn't look up; he was eyeing the man's boots when he spoke.

'Didn't recognize you from across the street ... from the sheriff's office,' the man said. 'But now I can see it's you ... underneath them whiskers, that is. You're Jubal Birch.'

Jubal suddenly felt the cold of the fading day. It made him shiver, and he took a long, deep breath.

'Close,' he responded, quietly, 'but the name's Oake.'

'I ain't changed as much as you, Birch. It should be easier for you to remember.'

The man remained very still as Jubal considered whether to look up. Jubal thought about his gun, back at the cabin, then he turned his head.

'If it's rememberin', it depends from where and when,' he drawled. 'You can walk, I can see that, and you seem to have all your arms an' legs. You musta been a friend. How'm I doin', stranger?'

The man was nervous, Jubal could see that. But he did remember, tried to recall the man's last words. They were to Margie, something like, 'They'll be back'.

And they were. The man now standing alongside Jubal was Luther Hose. Those who came back were Rouse Packman and the men from Pitchfork; the men who burned his home and killed Margie. Jubal stared hard at the man he'd once whipped near to death. His gut wrenched as he remembered the knife tearing at young Willum's ear.

Hose looked up and down the street. 'There's somethin' I need to discuss with you . . . some information I've got,' he said. 'We can go inside. You might need a drink . . . an' I might need witnesses.'

Jubal's eyes fixed icily on Hose.

'What the hell you talkin' about?' he said. 'You'll be lucky to get off this sidewalk alive with the whole of Yellow Pine watchin'.'

Jubal was trying to make sense of his thoughts and feelings as he got to his feet. Within moments, fifteen years didn't seem like such a long time.

'You're gonna find out pretty soon, Birch,' Hose said confidently. 'But I want to be the one to tell you. It's a business proposition. If you want to know what, follow me in.'

As Hose pushed through the doors of the saloon, Jubal clenched his fists. Angry and rattled, he followed Hose to the long bar, threw a quick glance around him.

'I don't know what the hell you're up to, Hose,' he hissed. 'The only business you an' me got is what I should've finished many years ago. What's to stop me doin' it right now?'

Hose thought for a second. 'Too many years an' the law,' he answered.

Hose grabbed at the bottle the bartender pushed across the counter. He poured into one of two glasses.

'I promised myself I'd hound you for the rest of my life for killin' my brother,' he said. He looked at Jubal, swallowed the whiskey in a single gulp.

'The rest of your life ain't too far off, you cowardly, murderin' scum.' Jubal felt his heart thumping, his temper breaking.

'Then neither's yours, Birch. My proposition . . . or should I say advice, should take care o' that.'

'What goddam advisin' you gonna give me, Hose?'

Hose disregarded Jubal's glass, poured himself another whiskey.

'My advice, Birch . . . or whatever you're callin' yourself now, is that you should buy up your little piece o' land along the river.'

'What are you talkin' about, Hose? How'd you find me? What the hell you doin' here?' Jubal was squeezing an empty glass, the knuckles of his big fingers stretched and white. He listened while Hose told him.

A year previous, after tiring of cattle life up in Oregon, Luther Hose had chanced up with Slur Tayter and Rosey Mangle in Cobre Wells. Mangle told him that he'd seen Jubal Birch; told Hose that the man who'd killed his brother had taken a wagontrain to the Powder River many years before. That conflict was something Hose was never going to forget, and fifteen years on he'd caught up with the man now known as Jubal Oake. But the days of laying waste, theft by force and gunfighting were drawing to a close. Luther Hose had to find another way – something that neighboured the law – to exact his mouldering retribution.

Jubal glared at him. 'After all these years, you're still interested in my land? You've got one minute, Hose, then I'll. . . .' Jubal's words trailed off. His jaw twitched and he slammed the glass hard against the counter.

Some of the confidence seemed to leave Hose as he recalled the power of the tough farmer's temper. He noticed one or two customers move uneasily away from the bar. He was unsettled now and smirked thinly as he pulled a folded piece of paper from an inside pocket. 'This is a deed. It's on the piece of land you're occupyin'.'

'What deed?' Jubal made a grab for the document, but Hose saw it coming and backed off a pace.

'This is only a copy. I've filed the original in Bakerville,' he said. 'Just read it, then you can destroy it . . . for all the good it'll do you.'

Jubal ground his teeth, reached for the document. He opened up the single sheet of paper and carefully read the words; with misgiving he tried to interpret the legal jargon. He looked at Hose, rising torment showing on his face.

'This says you're the owner of my land. How . . . where'd you get this?' he demanded.

'Where an' how don't matter. What does, is that it's legal . . . watertight. Your land does belong to me. Has done for a long week.'

Jubal laughed nervously. 'You want back at me, by tuggin' my rope. After all these years it's a long joke,

Hose. But I've stopped laughin', an' you've just about run outa time in this town.'

Hose shook his head. 'It ain't no joke, Birch. The purchase of land's a serious matter. You'll consider my offer before I leave town?'

'What offer?' Jubal scowled, impatient with anger.

'The offer of first refusal.' Hose measured his time, tossed down the whiskey. 'I'm plannin' to sell, an' offerin' you the chance to buy. It's a good deal . . . good land. If you're happy there, make me an offer.'

It was then that Hose's proposition got to Jubal – the truth of what was happening.

'Let me get this right,' Jubal said. 'You're tellin' me you own my land, an' you want me to buy it from you. Is that right?'

'Yeah. On the nail, Birch.'

'Now I understand,' Jubal said. He slowly released the whiskey glass, shook his head cheerlessly. 'Before I pay, you'll excuse me if I get this checked out?' he enquired of Hose as he tucked the paper under his shirt.

Before Hose answered, Jubal's hand closed around his throat. The pain was instant as he felt the crush. His arms and legs hung limp as his feet left the ground, and his bulging eyes came close to Jubal's enraged face.

'It was the most wrong thing my wife ever did, Hose, stoppin' me from killin' you,' Jubal rasped. He grabbed Hose's belt, twisted it tight and dragged him towards the saloon doors. He let go of Hose's neck and swung him forward, slamming his head into the batwings.

Hose fell on to the sidewalk and Jubal toe-rolled

him off, into the dirt of the street. The saloon customers were sensible enough to stay back, but Jubal's aggression attracted the attention of a few passers-by. Since Will Hammer had taken a grip on the town, street fights were a rare form of entertainment.

But like most of Jubal's contests, this was a one-sided event. The local folk sniggered as Jubal crossed the road, manhandled Hose along to the double-fronted hardware store.

From behind the big desk at the rear of his store, Moose Doogle was startled. He unclipped a pair of newly fashionable pince-nez spectacles and got to his feet.

'Jubal. What the...?' he began. He watched anxiously as Jubal swung Hose against stock-shelves.

'You know legal papers, Moose. At least you'll know a good one when you see it. Tell me about this.' Jubal held the paper out to Doogle. 'Read it,' he said.

Hose thought there might be some protection from a third party and yelled his indignation.

'I can have you arrested for this, Birch. There's witnesses. What I've done an' what I'm doin' now is legal.'

The dangerous look from Jubal quickly silenced Hose, who looked to Doogle for help. But Doogle wasn't about to offer any. He'd picked up on Hose's mention of the name, Birch, as he read the piece of paper. He remembered back to Cobre Wells and Jubal's interest in Rosey Mangle, the one-armed gambler.

'I'll be findin' out what you've done, Hose. An' if there's anythin' to it, it'll be the last thing you ever done,' Jubal threatened.

Hose saw the harm in pushing Jubal, rubbed at the pain in his neck.

Doogle raised his chin sharply at Hose.

'He's Luther Hose is he?' he asked Jubal.

'Oh yeah, no doubtin' that.'

Doogle refolded the paper. 'I know I didn't do it for you Jubal,' he said, 'but did *you* ever register your land . . . like I advised you to.'

Jubal looked uneasily from Doogle to Hose, back to Doogle.

'I told you I weren't gonna bother with no registering'. Anybody wantin' my. . . .' Jubal stopped for a moment. 'What you wanna know that for, Moose?' he added, hesitantly. 'That was four, maybe five years ago.'

Doogle patted his top pocket, feeling for a cigar.

'It's this document, Jubal. It's a copy all right, but the original says that Luther Hose is the legal owner of that piece o' land. Your piece o' land,' he said solemnly.

Jubal stood very still taking deep breaths. Hose was staring at Doogle, nodding with hopeful anticipation.

Doogle shook his head. 'I told you to get a government deed, Jubal. It was to prevent just this sort a thing from happenin'.'

Jubal looked confused and Doogle explained.

'The government made an enactment for settlers. Any one of 'em could stake out a section of land. All they had to do was make a register of it, an' it became theirs legally.' Doogle shook his head sadly, found his cigar. 'I remember tellin' you that, Jubal. Mr Luther Hose here, is a cunning fellow. He did what you should've, an' it's completely legal. You've been shafted by this thief, Jubal, an' I'd like to know why. You gonna tell me?'

'Yeah,' Jubal said. 'I shot his brother. The pair of

'em were runnin' me off my land. They mutilated my boy . . . crop-eared him. It was Hose's outfit killed my wife. It was a long time ago. What else you wanna know, Moose?'

'I'm sorry, Jubal, I had no idea. I guessed it was something, but. . . .' Doogle toyed with the cigar, rolled it between his fingers until the coin dropped. 'It was up here, wasn't it Jubal? That's how you knew Powder River country. You had to come back. It's why you brought the wagon-train,' he said, quietly putting it together.

Jubal was turned away, looking out through the glass-paned door. A blue norther was riffling the street. Within a few days the first snow would roll down from the mountains. It would get cold; freezing winds would search out every crack and nail-hole in every building in Yellow Pine.

Doogle bit off the end of his cigar, spat it into the floor.

'You shoulda gone to the sheriff's office, mister,' he said to Hose. 'You'd been a lot safer. You're wretched trash, an' I ain't gonna raise a finger to help you.'

Still looking out the door, Jubal asked distractedly, 'What do I have to do?'

Doogle sniffed. 'What would you have done, say fifteen, twenty years ago, Jubal? What would Jubal Birch have done?' he added cryptically.

Hose was edging along the shelves, his eyes rolling with fear.

'A fair price, Birch . . . it'll be a fair price,' he uttered.

Jubal turned on his heel, his insides churning with rage. 'I'll crush you. . . .'

Before Jubal got to him, Hose moved quickly behind Doogle's desk. Doogle himself thrust out an arm.

'No,' he shouted, his hand flattened against Jubal's chest. 'Think about it. What's your land worth?'

Jubal didn't answer, just stared silently at Hose.

'Think, Jubal.' Doogle continued. 'This louse is gonna say it's worth the life of his brother. What's that? What's his brother worth?'

'He was a spineless coward,' Jubal said, his intention unreadable.

He appeared to smile, then bent down to grab at something on the floor. He stood up and took two paces slowly towards Hose. He raised his hand and slammed it hard across Hose's mouth, up into his nose.

'That's the worth of you *and* your brother. A handful of sawdust and fly-shit. Now get out of Oregon before I kill you,' he rasped.

Doogle stepped forward and clutched at the long lapels of Hose's coat. He opened the door, and pushed him on to the sidewalk.

'Get away from here before Oake decides to settle up,' he snapped.

For the second time, Luther Hose had seen death in the man he knew as Jubal Birch. And he was scared as he hurried along the main street. Five minutes after Jubal had left Doogle's store, he was locked in his room in the small, false-fronted boarding-house at the south end of town. He'd waited a long time and still wanted revenge. He knew he'd try again, and the thought of it made him tremble.

16
Pitchfork Returns

Sam Kettle didn't waste much time in spreading the word. How the law had faced down Jubal Oake, the tyrant of the wagon-train from Cobre Wells. Quickly, the story spread throughout the town and along the Powder River.

Will Hammer hadn't said anything, it wasn't his way, but he heard the gossip. How the man once notorious for his belligerence, hardness and fighting ability had surrendered his gun. How Jubal Oake had turned his back on his home, ridden off without so much as a shaken fist.

There was no one, not even Moose Doogle, who knew of Jubal's whereabouts, or where he'd likely be headed. No one seemed that bothered, except the sheriff. At that time of the year, and with no weather break, Will Hammer knew you didn't go far with only a bedroll for comfort.

It was five days later when Jubal reappeared. When he walked into the Trail's End Saloon his eyes were sunken, and with his huddled, distressed appearance he went unrecognized. When he moved quietly to the bar and ordered a schooner of beer, no one noticed the .44 Colt tucked inside his jacket.

Jubal kept his head down, listened to the local talk. There was some excitement and some crude jokes, all of it centred around Bulldog Beattie.

Bulldog Beattie was actually Beatrice Bloom, a touring cantatrice, whom Moose Doogle had engaged to perform at Trail's End. But, like half a dozen other visitors and passers-through, she'd been delayed because of deep snow between Yellow Pine and the rail-head at Bakerville. She was famed throughout the northern states, allegedly gained her sobriquet from the way she handled the amorous advances of drunken cowboys.

Moose Doogle reckoned he was in for a handsome profit. The cost of one performance ticket was nearly as much as most folk earned in a month. But enough of them had dug deep, and Doogle was cramming in a few more lucrative performances.

Although Beattie was the object of much interest and animated vulgarity, not everyone in Yellow Pine was joining in. As Jubal stood at the bar, wrapped in his more ill-fated thoughts, he started at a voice close behind him.

'I don't reckon Jubal Oake's ever gonna turn up here,' a man proclaimed. 'He's a one-time notcher, gone yeller. That friend of mine waves a bit a paper, says "boo", and Oake just hands over his land drops his gun an' slinks off into the snow. Yessir, this Jubal Oake sounds like a real dangerous tiddy-cat to me.'

Jubal stared hard at the beer-ring on the counter in front of him. He tried to remember, tried to place the phrase and the man's voice.

The Landbreakers

'Yessir,' the man went on. 'Sounds more like the grit of a real hayshaker.' The man chortled, loudly demanded another whiskey. 'You tell me if you see him. I'll be stickin' around for a few more days 'til the snow clears.'

The man tossed back his whiskey and walked towards the swing doors.

A memory of a violent and painful brawl came back to Jubal.

'Hey mister,' he grated. 'Was that a tiddy-cat or a hayshaker made such a mess o' your face?'

It was the edge to Jubal's voice that sent a hush across the room. That, and because a few of the customers suddenly realized it was him, Jubal Oake, standing at the bar.

Jubal stood upright, took a small sideways step as he addressed the back of the stranger. Half-way to the swing doors, the man stopped and turned slowly, gave a long, penetrating look at Jubal.

'You,' he said simply.

It was Slur Tayter, one of those who'd run cattle along Strawberry Creek. After the fight with Jubal, he'd moved on from Dad Preeve's outfit, made himself a small reputation by fleecing settlers and landbreakers south of the Blue Mountains. Later, having to contend with law and order along the Powder River, he'd drifted a long way south, met up with Rosey Mangle and Luther Hose in Cobre Wells. It was there they'd talked about the man now known as Jubal Oake.

After ten, twelve years, the two men hardly recognized each other. Tayter was heavier than he had been, but still carried the scars on his face and the shattered nose from Jubal's beating.

Jubal looked calm, but his nerves were jangling. He could hardly believe it. Were they all back to get him? Were they all coming back for revenge, after what he'd done to them all those years before? Everyone had paid a high price for what had happened then; none more than Jubal.

But time had taken its toll. Jubal was tiring of the fight for a lone, peaceable life. A return match with Slur Tayter wasn't on his mind – unless he was pushed.

Tayter, though, had been surprised; it wasn't the way he'd planned the reunion. His gut churned and he felt muscle tension across the disfigurement of his face. But he'd been forced to live off his wits, and saw immediately that Jubal didn't appear to carry a gun. Perhaps, just perhaps, the man he once knew as Jubal Birch *had* been beaten, run off his land.

The adversaries locked eyes. It was something Jubal could walk away from again, but he wouldn't; it was too personal.

Slur Tayter had lost the advantage of taking Jubal unawares, and he felt sweat break across his scalp. He looked Jubal up and down.

'Don't look like you're up to handin' out punishment any more,' he managed without much faith.

The customers standing near to the bar backed off, others cleared a space between the two men. Jubal was aware that most eyes in the saloon were on him. It was too early in the day for Moose Doogle to be around, even tending to paperwork in his small, annexed office.

'You made the mistake of thinkin' that once before, Tayter,' Jubal snarled.

A vengeful smirk warped Tayter's mouth. He

stepped forward a pace, his stance challenging. 'That was then. Now's it's my time, hayshaker,' he snapped back.

Jubal seemed to sigh, but his eyes bore deep into Tayter.

'Well get on with it, Tayter,' he said. 'Or do I have to sweet-talk you into fightin' like I did last time.'

Inside the saloon, the stillness and silence was total when Jubal slowly pulled the big Colt from his jacket. Without taking his eyes off Tayter he set the action and placed it carefully on the bar counter beside him. He nodded imperceptibly at his adversary.

Tayter swallowed hard. With his right hand he pulled aside the flap of his range coat, revealed a Starr revolver holstered loose around his waist. As he felt his boldness seep away, he thought that maybe Jubal was full of bluff, maybe the big Colt was too high on the counter, maybe the hayshaker from Strawberry Creek *was* a tiddy-cat when it came to gunplay.

Maybe, he thought as he went for his gun. For a man going to fat, Tayter was quick. He managed to get his hand around the bone-handled butt, before Jubal's first bullet hit him high in the chest. The horror of pain didn't get to him until the second shot blew his neck apart. As he staggered backwards, he saw a cluster of ceiling lamps whirl around as he fell, tasted the blood as it filled his mouth. Before death brought on the crushing blackness, he even had time to ponder on the mistake he'd made; Jubal Oake probably had right on his side.

As the gunshots crashed and reverberated, Jubal fired again. Twice more he hit Tayter, watched coldly as the big bullets slammed home. 'That's it,' he said, 'you ugly son of a bitch.'

Through the hanging gunsmoke and acrid bite of powder, the clients of Trail's End stared; some at Jubal, some at the body of Tayter. Jubal put his gun back on the counter and motioned to the bartender, asked for another drink.

'Make it a whiskey – one of Moose's best,' he said.

The two men whom Tayter had been talking to were staring at the blood as it pooled into the dirt of the floor.

'Get him outside and find an undertaker,' Jubal advised them.

The men looked at each other. Tayter was a mess. He was shot to pieces and they were uncertain whether to carry or pull him from the saloon.

Jubal was about to tell them when Will Hammer shouldered his way through the batwing doors. He was closely followed by his deputies Sam Kettle and Big Carrow.

The sheriff immediately saw the body. From the grouping in the saloon, the set-up was obvious. He turned to Jubal.

'You came back for this, Oake?' he demanded. 'Brought your anger an' killin' ways into the town.' His eyes flashed angrily. 'Who the hell is this?' he asked, pointing his rifle at Tayter's body.

No one answered and he looked around the saloon. 'Who saw the shootin'?' he demanded, an intolerant edge to his voice.

Jubal thought of reaching for his Colt, but once again ceded to the corporal threat of Kettle and Carrow.

The man standing closest to Tayter spoke up.

'We saw what happened, Sheriff. The body here picked the wrong spot to start his slanderin'. What he was sayin' about Oake was sure provokin'.'

From there on, others joined in, pleased with their unanimous agreement in what had been fatally played out before them.

'So Oake shot him?' Hammer pressed.

'No, not then. Oake laid his gun on the counter ... about where it is now.'

Big Carrow flinched, levelled a shotgun at Jubal. Will Hammer shook his head.

The man who had spoken continued. 'Looked to me like he was offerin' it up ... not pushin' for a gunfight.'

The sheriff stared hard at Tayter's body, then he took a step towards Jubal.

'Hardly self-defence, but I could understand provocation,' he said, bitingly. 'I guess "extreme", would account for four bullets,' he added.

'He was one of a few men with a nasty habit of comin' back at me, Sheriff,' Jubal offered as an explanation. 'It's a long story. Perhaps one day you'll let me tell you about it.'

Will moved closer to Jubal. 'It was close to murder, an' everyone here knows it,' he seethed. 'That man's so fulla lead he's comin' to pieces. I did have some sympathy for what happened to you, Oake, an' I don't know if this man figured in it. But if you don't clear Yellow Pine, it'll be me tellin' *you* about the wooden hill.'

Jubal looked deep into Will's eyes. The fact that he was being run out of town by his own son was scary, freakish. He wanted desperately to say something to that effect, but he sensed the time and place to be far off, wondered if it always would be.

'I never wanted this to happen, Sheriff,' he said instead.

'Yeah, well what happens once can happen again. You're headin' for a one-way ride to Bakerville, Oake, an' I advise you to ride away now.'

'I ain't done nothin' wrong by the law, Sheriff. There ain't no reason to run me off.'

'You've come back for Luther Hose. I guess this man just got in the way. It's Luther Hose you want . . . I can smell it.' Will turned to look at his deputies, waved an arm to indicate getting Tayter removed.

Jubal reached carefully for his Colt. He stared at it for a moment, then pushed it back into his jacket.

Will rapped the barrel of his rifle against the bar.

'Remember, Oake. At this moment, Luther Hose is entitled to the protection of the law, an' that's me. If anythin' happens to him. . . .' The sheriff left his sentence unfinished.

Jubal pushed aside the empty beer-glass, downed the whiskey.

'Doubtless you'll come lookin' for me,' he concluded.

Will was about to say something else, but held back. He turned on those men who stood gawping as Kettle and Carrow struggled with Tayter.

'Help 'em for Chrissake!' he snapped.

Jubal turned away, looked tiredly into the mirror that ran behind the bar. He watched Will step over Tayter's body, push his way out through the batwings. He thought how different all their lives might have been if Margie had stayed with Willum that fateful night.

17
Yellow Pine

Within a week Jubal found his way out on to Moose Doogle's land. He had nowhere else to go, and travelling through the winter snows of Oregon was for bears and timber wolves.

He offered to work, to earn his keep, be stuck in Yellow Pine until early spring. But it wasn't so tough; it was precisely where he wanted to be. He was also close to the stretch he called his own, and the man who'd taken it from him: Luther Hose.

For old time's sake, Doogle offered up two hundred acres, but Jubal had his pride and turned it down. Besides, he wasn't for starting all over again. He'd had enough of land and owning things.

Late one night they were sitting in the comfort of Doogle's farmhouse. There were Indian sashes and wearing-blankets on the walls and a bearskin was spread across the floor. Jubal was sitting in a comfortable wing-back, rigging a tale as to why he was staying on in Yellow Pine. In turning down Doogle's offer of land, it was plain there was no purpose other than his wanting to keep an eye on Will Hammer.

'There's still somethin' I've got to settle, Moose,' he said. 'You know it, Will . . . Sheriff Hammer knows it an' everyone along the Powder River knows it. I'll be on my way when I've done.'

'Where to?' Doogle asked.

Jubal shrugged, started to make himself a cigarette. 'East, further north. Into Canada maybe.'

'That'll be after you've killed Luther Hose?' Doogle suggested, pensively.

Jubal tossed his cigarette makings into the big log fire, almost spat his response. 'I've got no family . . . other than a son who don't even know me . . . no job, no home an' no prospects. Hose is close enough to the reason for all of that. So yeah, you're damn right . . . after I've killed him.'

Most folk in the county *did* know that Jubal Oake would seek punishing damages from Luther Hose. The word around Yellow Pine was that Hose was prey to a persecuted and dangerous gun.

In the genuine hope of preventing a pointless death, Moose Doogle went to see Will Hammer. Doogle was a rich, influential businessman, and his profferings counted. He tried to talk the sheriff into heading off Luther Hose, but after listening to Doogle for only a matter of minutes, Will Hammer reached for his Winchester. He left his office, stamped through the snow that layered the sidewalk. Doogle was distressed. He wanted to tell Will Hammer that Jubal Oake was his father, but couldn't, and didn't really know why.

However it wasn't Jubal Oake whom Will sought out. As sheriff he thought he'd sorted that out, given plenty of warning. He knew where Luther Hose was, and it was to him he turned his attention.

The would-be landowner was keeping out of sight in the boarding-house at the end of town. As soon as Will slammed the door shut against the bitter cold, Theo Bunting twitched his head in the direction of one of the upstairs rooms.

The moment Will set eyes on Hose, he knew the man was aware of his own fate.

'You come to tell me you'll protect me, Sheriff? Is Oake comin' now?' he slavered.

Will gave a thin smile. Then, with one hand he dragged Hose from the chair he'd been sitting in.

'If I had my way, Hose, I'd break you across this chair,' he snarled. He pushed the tip of his Winchester hard under Hose's chin. 'The law says I gotta protect you, an' I'm havin' real trouble with that.'

'You can get me outa town, Sheriff,' Hose pleaded.

'Not in this weather, Hose. We're stuck in town.'

'There must be somewhere safe. Get me there.'

Will stepped back with a disgusted look on his face. 'There ain't a safe place for you, Hose . . . just a place. There's two rooms back of the Trail's End Saloon. Moose Doogle says it's where Bulldog Betty will be doin' her changin'. He says you can hole up there until she arrives.'

'Why's he say that? What's he wanna help me for?'

Will crossed the room, stared distractedly at the snowflakes as they brushed the window.

'Jubal Oake's had a time to stew. If he gets to you, he'll kill you,' he said. 'Then the law will have to step in. That's somethin' me an' Doogle don't want to happen.' The sheriff turned slowly, his eyes narrowed. 'That's why, Hose. Now get out of here, before I forget I'm the law.'

Hose's jaw dropped. 'You're comin' with me?' he asked, suddenly very frightened.

'Yeah, but Oake ain't in town . . . low life. If he was, you'd be dead already.'

Ten minutes later, they went through Moose Doogle's office into a store-room back of the Trail's End.

'When the snow clears, you can ride out to your new home,' Will taunted. 'In the meantime. . . .' Will didn't bother to complete the sentence.

Hose looked around him. 'I'll be alone here?' he muttered fearfully.

Will was contemptuous. 'I can't think of anyone who'd want to spend a moment in your company, Hose,' he said. 'My deputies will come an' get you when we know what Oake's up to.'

'You know what he's up to for Chrissakes,' Hose erupted.

Will had an urge to put a bullet into Hose himself. He'd be safe enough, Jubal Oake would only ever get the blame. He turned on his heel and stood in the doorway.

'Lock the door an' keep real quiet,' he sneered. 'If Jubal Oake so much as hears your teeth chatterin' he'll get a bullet into you.'

Will went off to find Moose Doogle. He'd be book-keeping in his hardware emporium.

'I've put him where you said. I guess he's safe enough . . . I didn't bother to check,' Will told him.

Doogle sat quietly, a little troubled, something on his mind.

'You gonna feed him?' Will asked. 'My office ain't runnin' to them luxuries.'

'He don't sound in much shape to eat, unless it's a

condemned breakfast.' Doogle almost smiled. 'I'll pay for it, if you get it to him. Reckon I'd be too scared to eat with Jubal Oake lookin' for me.'

'Yeah,' Will said. 'You reckon he'll turn up here?'

'What if he does, Will?'

'I'll have to stop him killin' Hose.'

'You'll arrest him?'

'I'll shoot him if I have to.'

Doogle swore, got quickly to his feet. He was getting red in the face, and his voice was breaking.

'For God's sake, Will, someone's gotta tell you. Tell you before it's too late.'

Will looked confusedly at Doogle. 'Too late for what?'

'Jubal Oake . . . or you.'

'What the hell you talkin' about?'

'His name's Birch . . . used to be Birch.'

Will looked bewildered. 'Birch?' he repeated the name.

'Yeah, the same name as you . . . before Hammer. He's your father, Will.'

Doogle was in now, and thought best to carry on. 'That man he killed in the saloon . . . he was one of those responsible for runnin' your ma an' pa off their land.'

For a moment, Will stood silent and motionless. He gripped his rifle tight. 'Who's Luther Hose?' he asked firmly.

'The brother of the man who took off part of your ear. Oake . . . your father, shot him 'cause of it.' Doogle lowered his voice to little more than a whisper. 'It was a long time ago Will . . . you weren't more'n a sprout.'

'I remember.' Will leaned against Doogle's big

desk. 'You'll have to tell me this again some other time, Moose,' he said quietly. He pulled the collar of his coat up and the brim of his hat down. He opened the door to the snow-swept street. 'He's my pa, you say . . . Jubal Oake's my pa,' he muttered. Then he walked into the chill, billowing whiteness.

With a lock turned and a bolt thrown, Luther Hose passed a fitful night in the Trail's End. It was well after first light that Big Carrow reluctantly handed him a plate of breakfast.

Hose found the daylight hours dragged slowly. The strain increased with the not-knowing whether Sheriff Hammer had detained or even got to Jubal Oake.

The long night hours brought their own cryptic terrors. He listened to the muffled bar-room sounds, occasionally heard raised voices, snatches of laughter, but it afforded him little comfort. He indulged in his own fearful company, contemplated the measure of grief he'd incurred since first arriving at Strawberry Creek with his brother.

Eventually another night turned into day, and with an early breakfast, Carrow had brought a single-page broadsheet. As Hose scooped up his warm beans with biscuit, he read of Beatrice Bloom and her appearance in Yellow Pine. Two columns described her charms and the allegory of her life. There was even a gauche illustration of her showing a long stockinged leg and satin garter.

Hose read the details avidly, studied the picture. For a while it took his mind off his own predicament. But he'd been deprived, and he felt curious, untimely resentment when he realized he wouldn't get to see her perform – maybe never.

He lay full length on the sofa, took turns in dozing and listening. It was sometime later the same afternoon that he heard loud noises from the bar-room.

He guessed it was Beattie arriving, maybe sharing a drink or two before her evening performance. Rubbing his arms against the chill, he stamped around the room a few minutes. He'd go out and see her. If Oake was there, he'd have to mingle with a few others by the sound of it.

Thinking he'd be safe enough, Hose unlocked the door to the office. As he stepped through the doorway, he froze when someone tapped gently on the door ahead of him, then shrank from the refrain of Bulldog Beattie's voice.

'Let me in, fella. It's as cold as a coon's nose out here.'

18
The Last Shot

From Moose Doogle's house it was nearly five miles into town. In the morning, Jubal had told Doogle he'd been thinking on his actions, not making any rash moves, ones that he'd regret. But now it was mid-afternoon and he'd got to the end of his ponderings. Besides, if he didn't do something quick, Luther Hose would get clean away.

He rode silent and remote. It was hard travelling, for the trail was hardly used. His mare had to flounder through deep, near impassable, drifts and the temperature was still dropping. Yellow Pine was blanketed in silence as he rode in from the south end, but although it was still fairly early there were lights strung out along the main street.

Leaving his mare outside the boarding-house, Jubal paid Theo Bunting a visit. It took a short explicit request to find out where Luther Hose was newly quartered.

Jubal walked further into town along the deserted sidewalk. Even allowing for the heavy snows, it was obvious that because of Beatrice Bloom there was a bigger crowd than usual in the Trail's End Saloon. Jubal turned down the side of the saloon, cautiously approached its narrow rear door. He paused for a moment, then tried the handle. Silent against the encrusted snow, the door opened into the saloon's store-room. Jubal made an acid smile. For all Hose's caution, he'd not thought to lock the door behind him, only the one in front.

From where he was standing Jubal could see a low light in the office that led off the store-room. Silhouetted against the glow, Jubal could make out a blocky figure. He guessed Hose was listening to sounds from the bar.

It would have been easy to put a bullet into the man, likely the smart thing to do. Hose would have – roles reversed. Jubal stepped cautiously forward around Hose's sofa. He leaned against the inner wall and, pulling the Walker Colt, pushed its long barrel against the glass. With his other hand he gripped the handle and twisted it quickly.

Directly in front of Jubal there was a brighter lamp that shone from the top of a writing-desk. As the wood of the door creaked, the figure turned sharply. but it was the cantatrice Beatrice Bloom who was alarmed, who shrank from Jubal's levelled Colt – Bulldog Beattie as she was known – not Luther Hose.

The sight of her took Jubal by surprise.

'Ma'am, I was expectin' someone else to be here,' he faltered.

'An' I was expectin' some privacy. Moose never said my room would be fulla men,' Beattie retorted.

Jubal didn't have much time to get the meaning of what Beattie was saying, and it was too late when he saw her eyes flick to a place behind him.

'Maybe it was me you were expectin' Mr Birch . . . or Oake, whatever your name is. Drop that hog-leg, and don't move. Don't even start to tremble.'

Hose's words sliced into Jubal. He was as guilty of carelessness as Hose in only thinking and looking ahead. He felt the gall in his mouth. If he dropped his Colt, he knew he'd get a bullet from a stressed, panicky man. It was the certainty of it that made him shake his head, and it was the wrong move.

Jubal turned as Hose pulled the trigger of his gun. He knew in an instant that Hose was never going to wait; not even until his own Colt hit the floor.

The blast of the shot fused with Beattie's gulping cry, and Jubal instinctively hurled himself sideways. He saw Beattie fall across the table, her body crushing the chimney of the oil-lamp on the desk

The room turned to instant blackness, but in the afterglow the scene was indelibly stamped. Luther Hose stood with fearful eyes and a smoking gun. He was staring at Beatrice Bloom who was spread grotesquely before him. Against the white of her bodice she appeared to be gripping a bunch of crimson flowers.

Jubal heard the warning click of Hose's gun-hammer, but his mind had retained the scene within the room. In one brief movement he dropped his Colt and hurled himself forward.

As Jubal's big hands grasped for the flesh and bone of Luther Hose, his mind flashed back to Strawberry Creek, Margie and young Willum. A wildness pounded through him as he made contact, as he prepared for a final and unforgiving fight.

He gripped Hose's gun-arm tight, smashed it left and right wildly until he heard the gun hit the floor.

He let go for an instant and managed to hook his arm around Hose's neck. He squeezed hard but got tripped and both men fell to the floor. Although in darkness, Jubal could tell he had the advantage. He was so close, he felt the man's dampness and the peppery sweat stung his nostrils.

After the gunshot, Jubal was expecting someone to come crashing through the door. But they were alone, thrashing blind and wild. It was for survival and both of them knew it.

Jubal felt a brief slackness in Hose before fingers tore cruelly at his face. He rolled on to his back and lashed out with his feet, at the same time grabbing and pulling with his hands. His feet made a more solid contact, and with a crash and splintering of glass the door of the office flew open.

Locked together, the two men were turned into the far end of the bar-room. The customers had heard Hose's gunshot all right, but none of them was prepared to look into it. They were only interested enough to form a broad horseshoe around the door to Moose Doogle's office; the room Bulldog Beattie was using as he changing-room .

Jubal quickly twisted away to give himself an advantage. Swearing excitedly, he pushed himself to his feet. Then he was up and running, his eyes a sweeping challenge to the startled, suddenly frightened onlookers. He made the end of the long bar just as the bullet smashed into his leg above his left knee. He gasped at the pain, swore again. It was Hose. He'd been carrying a belly-gun in the band of his pants.

Jubal threw himself behind the bar. The bartender paled and backed off, dropping his glass-cloth. He held out his hands in fearful sufferance as Hose's second bullet ripped into the bar-front. As Jubal hit the floor, he pointed to the running-shelf along the inside-back of the bar. Jubal nodded, twisted up and made a grab for the sawed-off shotgun.

The bartender was now crouched at the far end of the bar. Jubal held up the gun and gave him a penetrating look. The bartender nodded convincingly and Jubal knew the shotgun was loaded. He got to his knees, flinched with pain as he poked the barrel over the bar. He tipped it upwards, towards a cluster of lamps that was lighting the room, thumbed back the hammers.

'You're gonna burn in Hell, land-grabber!' he yelled, as he pulled one of the triggers.

The overhead lights went out in a downpour of shattered glass and oil. As the boom from the shotgun reverberated around the saloon, Jubal aimed at the second cluster. He gave them the second barrel, and within moments the bar was suffused with the hot taint of oil. those men who hadn't made it through the doors were cowering against the walls, their senses reeling from the conflict.

There were more cartridges in a cardboard box and Jubal reloaded. He looked up at the high shelves that ran along the back mirror. There were some cut glasses and they twinkled brightly under the one remaining cluster of hanging lights. Fancy labels adorned the bottles, and for a moment Jubal supposed business had got real good for Moose Doogle. Then he wondered about Hose. There was no more shooting, and he couldn't hear much above the background clamour.

Quickly, he lifted the shotgun again and pointed both barrels along the counter-top. This time there was real terror. Jubal felt it himself as the gun blasted, the buckshot sweeping everything from the counter, the yelling as a thousand fragments of glass and liquor overwhelmed the room.

In the confusion, Jubal pushed out from the end of the bar. He swung the shotgun to where he guessed Hose to be, but he wasn't there. The saloon was empty. Everyone had left. The batwing doors had stopped moving.

But he knew Hose hadn't got out. This time it would be to the finish. Hose wouldn't have wanted it that way, but he'd know it had to be, he'd know he wasn't getting out alive.

Jubal's leg was an unbearable mass of pain as he rolled his way back to behind the end of the bar. Now it was going to take more than a single shot, and he'd need another cartridge.

Hose took the barrel of his belly-gun from hard against the bartender's neck and fired low along the back bar. He'd got into position and waited for Jubal, fired the instant he'd seen him.

The bullet drilled, burned into Jubal's shoulder and he went over. But Jubal had seen the flicker of movement. He'd already slammed the shotgun down into the crook of his arm and jerked at the twin triggers. He fell on to his back and took a few shallow breaths. He didn't need to look at what he'd shot.

Luther Hose didn't feel any pain, he was beyond that. From such close range, Jubal's shot had destroyed most of his senses. But he could smell. Through the blood and gore that covered his face, the scene of Bulldog Beattie fluttered around the remains of his nose: A bizarre fragment of reality, before agony hammered him into oblivion.

His face grey and sweating with pain, Jubal managed to change the spent cartridges. With his good leg he pushed himself away from the bar. He made it to the doorway of Doogle's office, then he could go no further. He twisted his head to look back into the room, dimly saw Beattie's body slumped and unmoving across the littered desk.

Then he turned back to the bar-room. He gritted his teeth, grinned darkly at the finger of flame. It was running towards the coal-oil that flowed thin and threatening across the floor of the saloon.

19
Reunion

Theo Bunting pushed open the door of the sheriff's office. He found Will Hammer and Moose Doogle talking with the deputies. The heavy snows would keep any trouble off the street and they were sharing a drink before going to see Beatrice Bloom at the Trail's End. It was at Doogle's invitation, and Sam Kettle was joshing, bending a proverb.

'It's an ill blizzard that blows nobody no good. I sure am lookin' forward to seein' that garter of Miss Bloom's.'

Big Carrow chuckled. 'We'll go an' quieten 'em down before the show starts. Sounds like some of 'em are already shootin' the roof off Mr Doogle's saloon.'

The men looked up, grimaced at the snowflakes and cold that blew in with Bunting.

Will eyed the man from the boarding-house.

'Run into someone's fist, Theo?' he asked, noticing the bruise under Bunting's eye.

'Yeah, that's what I come to see you about. It was Jubal Oake. He woulda done more if I hadn't told him.'

Short-lived content disappeared from the sheriff's face.

'Jubal Oake. You seen him in town? Where? What you been tellin' him?'

Bunting looked miffed at the lack of concern for his hurt. 'He came bustin' into my place . . . wanted to know where Hose was,' he answered.

'An' you told him?' Kettle interrupted.

Bunting took off his fur cap, pushed his face close to the deputy.

'Yeah, I told him,' he said sourly.

Will was out from behind his desk, reaching for a coat.

'When was this?' he asked anxiously.

'No more than an hour ago.'

Wills face clouded over. 'Why didn't you get here sooner?'

'I came as soon as I could. What's it matter to you?'

Doogle was the only one to understand Will's concern. 'Because he's the sheriff, that's why,' he snapped.

'Moose, you come,' Will said. 'I'm afraid of what. . . .' He stopped, changed the direction of his thoughts. 'It's your place, goddammit,' he offered instead.

On the sidewalk outside his office Will stared through the falling snow. Away on his left he saw two men staring across the street. One of them looked up and waved, jabbed his hand excitedly at the Trail's End.

Carrow winked at Kettle.

'That shootin' weren't high jinks Sam. Jubal Oake's gone too far this time. Will's gonna have to kill him I reckon . . . told him he would.'

Will swore, took off at a run and the other followed. Doogle was alongside Big Carrow.

The Landbreakers

'Hundred dollars says you're wrong,' he said.

Along the street there were a few oil-lamps throwing eerie, yellow pools of light across the deep snow. The town appeared to be deserted, the only sound in the blue dark was the muffled thump of Will's boots as he took the steps of the saloon.

As he burst through the swing doors, he saw his father through the sweep of orange flames. Jubal was at the far end of the saloon propped against the doorway. His head was back and he was staring up at the shattered lamp-carriers.

'He's hurt, Will. Where's Hose?' Doogle was breathless as he pushed up behind the sheriff.

Will pointed his rifle at Hose's feet which poked from the near end of the bar.

'Grabbin' another piece o' land,' he said viciously. He looked over at Jubal. 'Ain't gonna be long before these flames get to you, Oake. I told you about Hose . . . gave you forty-eight hours. Seems you're always givin' me problems.'

Jubal spoke quietly. His chin fell to his chest, his fingers let go of the shotgun.

'What's your beef this time, Sheriff?'

'Do I leave you lyin' there, or do I come an' get you?'

'As you say, Sheriff . . . you're the one with the problem.'

Will anxiously watched as the flames soared further across the saloon. He turned to his deputies.

'Get round the back. You can reach him through Moose's office,' he snarled.

'Where the hell's Miss Bloom?' Doogle shouted at Jubal. 'You seen her?'

'She never made it outa your office, Moose. Hose

made sure of that. That makes *him* the killer.' Jubal tried an exasperated smile.

Will shook his head, looked at Doogle.

'I can take care of this,' he said. 'Go get some help if you want your building from burnin' down.'

Doogle nodded thoughtfully, backed off through the swing doors.

'We're on our own, Sheriff. Better make up your mind what you're gonna do with me,' Jubal croaked.

'I ain't gonna shoot you, an' I ain't gonna let you burn to death. Not my own pa.' Will took a step closer, held up his hand against the heat of the rising flames. Through the hiss and crackle he heard a short, gurgling laugh.

'I knew Moose would tell you . . . just didn't know when. It's the timing, Will . . . I never did get it right.'

Will was wondering how long it would take Kettle and Carrow to get to Jubal. 'You don't wanna stick around there, Pa. I'll give you time to get to your horse,' he came up with.

'In this weather, you kiddin'? Anyways, I've lost so much blood, the crawl there'd kill me.' Jubal closed his eyes against the tiredness and pain. 'Besides,' he said, 'you don't really want me to leave now, do you, son? Not now we've got the town tamed.'

'No, Pa, not now,' Will said, as he saw his deputies appear through the back office.

20
Second Chance

Jubal Oake sat uncomfortably on a deckchair at the end of town. The gunshot wounds had been effectively doctored, but his whole body ached. It was still bitterly cold and he shivered under blankets and a fur skin.

Where Trail's End had burned to the ground, black charred stubs poked through the snow that still lay clean across the land. Some said the fire was God's reckoning, others that it gave Moose Doogle an excuse to build a bigger, more elaborate, saloon with a proper theatre and dance hall.

Will Hammer stood on the sidewalk, his arms wrapped around him against the chill.

'I don't rightly know what to call you . . . now.' He stumbled through his sentence.

'Yeah, must be difficult. But *rightly*, it's still Pa.' Jubal coughed, laughed, pulled at his blanket.

Will stamped his feet. 'There was something I meant to tell you,' he started. 'About that old dog o' yours. . . .'

Jubals eyes flickered. 'What about him?' he asked.

'When Carrow went into your cabin that time . . . he was dead . . . the dog. Carrow said there was still some warm to him. Musta died the minute you left.'

Jubal stared into the distance, squinted at the brightness.

'Yeah I know how he felt,' he said distractedly. 'Shame about him . . . an' Miss Bloom.'

Will nodded. 'Never seen so many folk gathered.'

'There was silence for a full minute before Jubal said anything else. 'Moose ever tell you why she was called Bulldog Beattie?'

'Yep, he did,' Will answered.

There was another long pause, and Jubal tried again. 'Bet you don't remember what I told you about snow.'

Will laughed. 'I do. Poor man's fertilizer, you said it was.'

'Yeah, that's right.' Jubal sniffed loudly, stopped his mind from wandering back. 'Ain't got a lot to say, have we?' he added.

'I'd say there's plenty, but this ain't the time. Right now there's a heap of work needs doin'. Some of it out at that stretch of land along the Powder River. Take the two of us, I reckon.'

Jubal suddenly felt less cold. 'The land don't belong to me,' he reminded Will.

'Luther Hose left a confession somewhere . . . sort of last will and testament. Doogle's lookin' . . . he'll find it.'

Jubal understood and looked up at his son. He grinned.

'A resourceful man, Moose Doogle.' After a moment he went on to say, 'About Luther Hose. . . .'

Will cupped a gloved hand around his scarred ear.

'Yeah, I know,' he said. 'Ma told me.'

There was another, even longer, silence.

'Did you bury the old hound?' Jubal asked eventually.

'Yeah,' Will answered. 'I done a lot of buryin' recently.'